CHAPTER ONE

They killed him in Spangle Valley. They waited hidden among the rocks on Buffaloback Mountain and when he rode below they shot him out of the saddle.

Far up the pass, where the mountains reared into a jagged line against the sky, the men at Bancroft Roadhouse stopped what they were doing as they heard the distant shots. The faint, angry cracking of rifles was answered briefly by the blunt roar of a heavy revolver, and then there was nothing more to hear.

The whip on the Yellowrock-Carolville stagecoach had one foot out on the rim of the front wheel. When the whispering echoes had died away, he jumped to the dusty ground in front of the roadhouse, and his passengers started getting out of the coach.

A little old man wearing a black suit and hat was the first to step down. He straightened his square-cut glasses and said, 'You know what that shooting was, driver?'

The whip shrugged. 'Likely some fellow shot hisself a deer.'

The second passenger was holding a nearly empty bottle, and he almost fell out of the stage. He was a tall young man with blue eyes and black, wavy hair that curled out from under his white stetson. He wore a soft gray shirt with white stitching around the pockets and there was a thin, store-bought kerchief of red silk around his throat. His heavy black cartridge belt was elegantly scrolled in Mexican silverwork, and it held two pearl-handled Colts in rich holsters.

He said, 'Deer, hell! You got no sense of timing. I'll put five dollars to four somebody just got bushwacked.'

The coach rocked under the step of the next man out. A powerfully built giant of a man, he dropped heavily to the ground and grunted, 'You're so damned smart! Think you can tell what's bein' shot at when you ain't even there!' He wiped his mouth with his sleeve. 'I'll take that bottle, Cash.'

5

Cash moved back out of the giant's reach. He lifted the bottle and finished it, then held it out toward the big man and laughed. 'Pleasure to give you the bottle, Ben.'

Ben grabbed the bottle angrily. 'Right now, I'm gonna shove this down your throat!'

'Hold it, Ben!' The last man off the stage was dark and slender, with a tight, thin mouth matched by a scratch-line of a mustache. From the quick, graceful way he moved, seeming to hold nervous strength and high speed just barely under control, he looked like a man-sized wasp. 'Plenty more whisky inside. No point fightin' over it.'

The driver said, 'We'll change horses here. Be pullin' out for Yellowrock in about twenty minutes.'

The station attendant approached the stage as the passengers walked toward the roadhouse. The driver nodded at him and glanced down toward Spangle Valley. 'Holdup, maybe?'

'Nah. The Y-C coach ain't due yet. But a man named Sullivan rode outa here alone, quarter of an hour ago. He'd of been somewheres around Buffaloback about now.'

'Sullivan? Fellow that's supposed to be Yellowrock's new sheriff?'

'Yeah.' The attendant slapped at a horsefly on his neck. 'Just about got your team harnessed.'

'Good. Be glad when this run is over. Duke and Big Ben ain't no fun under any circumstances, and that fancy dressed young fellow's been tryin' to get hisself killed. Been funnin' Big Ben and drinkin' the road dry all the way from Tucson.'

The fresh team was hitched to the Yellowrock coach when the Concord bound for Carolville came lurching up the pass toward Bancroft, its wheels rumbling swiftly at the head of billowing clouds of dust, its thorough-braces squealing under the wrench and strain as eight sweating, galloping horses lunged against their collars.

'Get Hibby!' the driver yelled as the stage rolled to a stop. 'Got a man hurt! Maybe dead!'

The blacksmith named Hibby ambled stolidly from the stable while the men in the coach carried a limp body into the roadhouse.

Inside, they lined two tables together and stretched the

Huffaker

Badge for a Gunfighter

Futura Publications Limited

A Futura Book

First published in Great Britain in 1974
by Futura Publications Limited

Copyright © 1957 by Clair Huffaker

ISBN 0 8600 7040 9
Printed in Great Britain by
Hazell Watson & Viney Ltd
Aylesbury, Bucks

man out on them. 'Picked him up off the road,' the shot-gun rider said. 'You're fair at fixin' horses, Hibby, so we brung him along for you to look at.'

The blacksmith leaned down and studied a small, round hole in the man's vest, which was now caked with blood. He listened for a heartbeat, then licked his finger and held it next to the man's lips. After a moment he said, 'He ain't bleedin', his heart ain't beatin', and he ain't breathin'. He's plain dead.'

There was a tiny, choking sob from the doorway. A boy about nine years old was standing there staring at the body on the table. When the men turned to look at him he moved quickly out of sight. The little man in the square-cut glasses followed after him.

Cash, leaning back against the bar with a drink in his hand, grinned at Big Ben and the slender man named Duke. 'Like I said, Ben. Fellow got bushwhacked.'

Outside, the little man saw the boy sitting on the step of the Carolville coach. He walked over and touched the youngster softly on the shoulder. 'What's the trouble, son? You kin to the man?'

'No, sir. I found him. I was fishin' in the creek and heard the shootin' and went up and found him.' He wiped his eyes with the back of his hand and stared down at his scuffed brogans. 'He knew he was dyin', and he was worried about how I'd feel havin' him die on my hands. He was talkin' normal, and I was tryin' to talk some life into him but I couldn't think of the right things to say.' The boy choked back another sob that came from deep down.

'Any idea who shot him?'

'No, sir.'

The little man rubbed his chin with his thumb as the Carolville driver joined them by the coach. 'Strange. Hadn't even got into town. Hadn't a chance to make an enemy.'

The driver watched the stable hands unhitching his tired team. 'Point is,' he said, almost to himself, 'he was gonna be sheriff. There are folks who'd take a dislike to him on no more'n them grounds.'

'I see.'

'Certain folks get a town under their thumb, they don't

7

like to see no lawmen or preachers or politickers or what-all comin' around, tryin' to change the way things are.' The driver glanced at the roadhouse where the other three passengers for Yellowrock were coming through the door. He lowered his voice. 'You take them three. Duke and Big Ben are two old-timers who work for Whitey Hall. And I expect the new fellow will maybe be goin' to work for him. Whitey's the biggest man in Yellowrock. He wouldn't like to see no change at all.' He paused. 'Truth is Hall even owns the line I'm drivin' for, and I talk too much.'

The driver turned to the boy. 'Kid, you go up to that Yellowrock coach there. Old John's whip on 'er. He'll take you into town or drop you off anywheres along the way if you want.'

'Much obliged.'

The little man and the boy walked toward the Yellow-rock coach. As the three men ahead of them got to the stage, Big Ben suddenly bellowed, 'By hell! I took enough a your big talk, Cash! If you don't think I can whip you, you can just prove it right here and now!' He shoved Cash hard.

The young man slammed drunkenly into the paneled coach door and weaved back, laughing at the big man. 'You're a ton and a half of muscle and a quarter-ounce of brain, Ben. Naturally I can whip you, but I'd have to damn near kill you to do it.'

'You won't fight?' Ben asked.

'Nope.' Cash couldn't seem to stop laughing. 'You're too dumb for me to be mad at you.' He staggered to keep his balance. 'Besides, it wouldn't be a fair fight. You're drunk.'

Ben glanced around. His eyes came to rest on an old wagon wheel with three spokes missing. He roared, 'Damn! You ain't got the spit to stand up and fight. I'll show you!' Stumbling to the wheel, Ben picked it up in one hand. Grasping an ash spoke in his right hand, he heaved against it. Nothing happened at first. He set his head at a lower angle and heaved again. His panting breath stopped as his muscles reached their greatest tension. A thin, whispering sound gave way to a slow splintering and then a loud crack as the spoke snapped in the middle.

8

Ben looked up and yelled triumphantly, 'There! You think you're so almighty much!' He rolled his massive head at Cash. 'Come on over here and let's see you do a man's chore like that!'

Cash put his hands on his lean hips and shook his own head loosely, in contemptuous imitation of the man who stood thirty feet away holding the wheel.

'Now that's exactly what I mean. All that mountain of beef and no figuring ability whatsoever. You want to break a spoke in a wheel, here's how.'

Cash pulled a gun and shot a spoke out of the wheel between those last two words. The thunder of the gun's blast was mingled with the sound of the shattered spoke whipping through the air.

Ben yelped and jumped away from the wheel. 'You almost hit me!' he bellowed furiously. 'I felt the bullet pass me by!'

Cash grinned happily. 'You ain't hurt.'

Much soberer, Ben said, 'For all your braggin' and trick shootin', I could tear you in half.'

'No harm done yet,' Duke said crisply. 'Let's forget it.'

The big man said nothing, but stamped into the coach so that it tipped under his angry step.

'I want another drink, Duke,' Cash said.

'Whitey's waitin' on us. We'd best get goin'.'

The C-Y driver came out of the roadhouse and said, 'If it's okay with you boys, let's roll.'

Cash shrugged his shoulders and said, 'All right, I'll have that drink in Yellowrock.'

The little man helped the boy into the stagecoach and they sat facing the three men. The driver's whip snapped up ahead and the team lunged forward.

Cash grinned at the boy and said, 'Ben, I'll lay you ten dollars this kid can whip you. Bare knuckles. First one can't get up loses.'

The big man growled at Cash and shot a murderous look at the boy. Scared and embarrassed, the youngster dropped his eyes.

'I'd leave the boy alone,' the little man said in a firm voice. 'He's had a bad day. He found the man who was ambushed.'

Cash said, 'Okay. I was just kidding Big Ben here.'

Ben slouched his huge shoulders into the corner of the seat. 'Some day you'll stop laughin'. Some day I'll twist that neck of yours like a chicken's.'

Duke, sitting between them, said, 'Once was a gun-slinger up north name of Jack Slade. They tell me the drunker he was the better he could shoot.'

'Hell, I shoot better when I'm sober,' Cash told him. 'Cold sober I can shoot my own bullets right out of the air. Trouble is, it all happens so fast nobody but me can see it.'

Duke muttered, 'There's others could make that shot you just made. So don't get too big for your britches. And,' he added dryly, 'the real test of shootin' comes when some-one's shootin' back at you.'

Cash grinned, leaned back, and tilted the white stetson down over his eyes. He was soon asleep.

After a long silence, the little man said to the boy, 'Feeling any better?'

'Yes, sir.' The youngster looked at the men across the narrow aisle. Ben was now asleep too, a deep, threatening snore rumbling far down in his chest. Duke's eyes were open, but cold and blank, as though his mind had turned in on itself.

'What's your name, son?'

'Hank, sir. Hank Brendan.'

'Mine's Williams. Try not to let it hit you too hard.'

'Well, Mr. Williams, I guess it's just that he was so – so much a man. He had eyes that looked right inside a fellow, but still they were friendly, somehow. I – I just can't – It's hard to think of him dead.'

Williams waited a minute, then switched the talk around. 'What kind of a town is Yellowrock? Big?'

'I'll say.' Hank nodded his head. 'Got more houses than you can count. Got three hotels, six or eight stores, lots of stables and saloons. It's plenty big.'

'Got schools or churches?'

'No school. They started a church about two years ago, but never did finish buildin' it.'

'Too bad. People ought to have a church to go to.'

'Not me. I don't go for that stuff.'

'Why not?'

10

'When the Mescaleros got Dad, the preacher was scared and wouldn't come out from town. Mr. Reny, down the road, said a prayer and we buried him. Five weeks later, when the army was thick as flies in the territory, the preacher finally come out. Ma told that preacher if he was a sample of what the Pearly Gates had to offer, then folks had got the Devil and God mixed up over the years. She made him leave our house. Then she sat down and cried.'

'She did right,' Williams said.

'That preacher was scared of everythin'. We got no use for his kind.'

The sun was low in the west when they reached the far end of Spangle Valley.

'I'd be obliged if I could get off here,' Hank said. 'Our place is just over the hill.'

Mr. Williams called to the driver to stop and helped Hank down from the coach.

'Much obliged,' Hank said. 'I'm pleased to've met you.'

'I'll be calling at your house.'

'You will?'

'I'm a preacher by trade. Going to try my hand at Yellowrock.'

The boy's jaw fell and his lips parted. 'Well, good luck – sir.'

The coach rolled on down the road, picking up speed as it went.

CHAPTER TWO

Cash Jefferson opened his eyes to find Duke shaking his shoulder in the dark coach, as the little man in the opposite seat started to climb out the door.

'Wake up. We're here.'

In the other corner, Ben was beginning to stir. Cash yawned and leaned forward. Once down from the stage, he walked a few steps in the dark shadows of the side street the coach had pulled into. Facing him was a broad thoroughfare lined with several gaily lighted, noisy saloons. Through the open batwing doors of the Oriental Saloon across the way, he could see a milling crowd of men and women. The men were solid walls of gray, black and mud-colored clothes. The women who occasionally moved in and out of his line of vision were flamboyant splotches of yellow, purple, green and red against the dull male background. A piano tinkled an enthusiastic 'Oh, Susanna' over the loud voices, shouts and laughter.

Duke joined Cash with the giant Ben in tow. 'Ben's like a grizzly,' he grumbled. 'Hard to wake up.'

'What about my warbag?'

'Driver'll have a boy take your stuff over to the Holiday Hotel.'

Duke started back along the alley, with Ben shuffling behind. Cash fell in with Duke, who said, 'We're goin' around the back way. Whitey'll be in the office at the Alamo. One of his places.'

The second building on their left was the Alamo. Ben slumped into a chair inside the back door and said, 'I ain't feelin' so hot.'

Cash shook his head. 'You better learn not to drink along with an expert, sonny.'

Ben glared at him.

Duke said, 'Try a hair of the wolf that bit you. The boss wants to talk to Cash personal anyway.'

Through a curtain drawn over an archway, Cash could hear people in the crowded saloon beyond. Duke knocked at a heavy door farther to the rear of the building and some-one called, 'Yeah?'

'Duke. With the new man.'

A bolt slid back and the door was opened. Cash went in behind Duke. Three wooden-faced, narrow-eyed men were standing in the room. One wore a brown sling on his arm.

At the ornate desk in the center of the room sat a blond man with hard brown eyes and a scar that ran along his cheek and up to the bottom of his right ear. This, Cash knew, was Whitey Hall.

'Well,' Whitey said. 'I've been waiting for you.' He motioned to the three men. 'You boys go on out to the bar.'

When they were gone, Whitey turned to Cash. He smiled and said, 'So you're Cash Jefferson?'

Cash considered the question briefly. 'I guess in all modesty I have to admit you're right.'

'What do you think of him, Duke?'

'Don't like him. And Ben's all set to break him in half over his knee.'

'What's wrong with him?'

'He gets under your skin. Talkin' to Ben through his hat about being able to whip him. And he was showin' off up to Bancroft with a gun – shot a spoke out of a wheel,' Duke said disdainfully.

'Could you have shot it out, Duke?' Whitey asked.

'Easy. You just gotta catch the spoke right at the skinny part by the hub.'

'What about you, Cash? What do you think of my two employees?'

'Nothing.'

'Duke here,' Whitey said mildly, 'is generally believed to be the best gunfighter west of St. Louis. I know damned well you've heard plenty about him. Ben used to be a circus strong man. Between them they could take on half the town. And you think nothing of them?'

'Well, I guess I do think one thing about them. They're lousy company.'

Whitey's lips twisted into a thin smile. 'I'm glad to hear that. As long as the gentlemen working for me don't enjoy each other's company too much, their only loyalty is to me. Right, Cash?'

'My only loyalty is to cash.'

'How do you mean that?'

'Both ways. Myself and money. That's how I got the monicker in the first place.'

'You've got quite a reputation, all right.' Whitey produced a bottle and glasses from a drawer. 'Drink?'

'I've been dying of thirst.'

Whitey poured whisky into two glasses. 'Duke doesn't indulge.'

Cash moved across the room and sat on the desk. 'Can't say I blame him. Alcohol's hard on the nerves. Don't imagine his could stand much.'

Duke flipped open his coat so that his walnut-handled Smith & Wesson was in easy reach. His face was hard and angry. 'Now's the time to find out about my nerves.'

'Forget it!' Whitey's voice cracked in command. He continued in a lower tone. 'Now here's the proposition, Cash. You can make more money than you ever knew existed. But you can't deliberately antagonize my men, or you'll never live to spend it.'

Cash said, 'Thanks for tipping me off. I'm too young to die.'

'Now let's get down to business,' said Whitey. 'I know almost as much about you as you know about yourself. You're twenty-eight, given name Bruce Jefferson. Born on a farm in southern Illinois. Family wiped out during a Confederate raid. Lived with an uncle in Ohio. Ran away and went to Texas to be a brush popper. Killed a man in San Antonio. Went on the prod. Killed three men since then.'

'Five,' Cash corrected him. 'Couple didn't get written up in the newspapers.'

'Anyway, you were cleared in the shootings that did get public attention. Lawmen aren't chasing you.'

'They wouldn't dare.' Cash grinned.

'As far as people are concerned, if they've ever heard of you at all, they figure you're an argumentative person with a better than average gun hand. But the truth is that your run-ins were simple hired killings.'

Cash shrugged. 'You might say I'm a gambler at heart. A certain party might bet me five hundred dollars that I

14

can't outdraw another party. If I win I'm ahead five hundred. If I lose I'm dead.'

'The men you've killed so far have been gunfighters themselves. Out of curiosity, if the bet was, say, shooting a man in the back, would you take it?'

Cash grinned. 'Just simpler to win. I don't reckon the other fellow's much happier one way or the other. Forward or backward, he's just as dead.' He poured another drink. 'Want a refill?'

'Yes.' Whitey watched as the steady, bronzed hand poured a second tumbler of gold-brown liquid. 'I like to see a man who hates people. That's a man you can count on.'

'Why, I don't hate anybody in the whole wide world, Whitey. I just don't gave a damn about them. Let's cut out all this palaver. What's the deal?'

'I'm figuring on making you sheriff of Yellowrock.'

Cash gagged slightly on his whisky and put the glass down sharply. 'You've got a sense of humour after all,' he said, and coughed.

'Nothing funny about it. I'd like to have Duke in the job, but everybody knows he's my man. I imported you because no one knows you around here. You can take over, and the town will be tickled pink. But you'll enforce the laws the way I want them enforced and you'll gun anyone I want you to gun – and always perfectly legally.

'The job pays one-fifty a month. I'll match it with one-fifty on my own payroll. The job pays two dollars a head for any cowboys or miners you jail in the line of duty. Just to encourage you to look like a conscientious officer, I'll match that money, too. We want you making plenty of arrests. But make sure you don't bother me or my men or anyone spending his pay in one of my places. And, from time to time, you'll get a bonus for special jobs.'

'What sort of special jobs?'

Whitey leaned back in his chair and put his hands behind his head. 'Remember the three men who were here when you came in? They did a little extra work for me today. So they've got a thousand dollars to split up between them.'

'For that kind of money I'm your sheriff. What job did they do?'

'Fine. You're one of us.' Whitey saluted Cash with his whisky glass. 'Those three discouraged a lawman from taking over the sheriff's office. You were my choice, so I had to make room for you.'

'The corpse we picked up at Bancroft?'

'That's the one. People got up a town council a while back. They hired this man without my say-so while I was in San Francisco on a business trip. I knew Sullivan – that was his name – in Kansas City. He knew my record, a record I could still serve time on if they ever found me. Maybe Sullivan suspected I was in Yellowrock, maybe not.' Whitey drummed his fingers on the desk top. 'In any case I couldn't take chances.'

Cash put his empty glass down and stuck his thumbs in his belt. 'I can see gunning Sullivan. But why go to the trouble of installing your own man as sheriff?'

Whitey waved his hands out, palms up. 'Simple. Same as with you, money is my guiding light. I own five of the town's eight saloons, and a few other properties. I own part of the Lucky Bronco silver lode – one of the mines that keeps this town going. Two thirds of the wages earned around here come straight to me over my faro and black-jack tables. I'm a monopoly in Yellowrock, and I like it. I like it so far about a million dollars' worth. With a setup like that I want to take no risks.'

'And just in passin',' Duke said, breaking his silence, 'any trigger-happy saddlebum tries to play games with Whitey, he don't live long after.'

'What Duke means is that I'm not telling you this lightly, Cash. Working for me is a lifetime contract.'

'How do you make me sheriff? Just pin a star on me?'

'That's about all there is to it. I'm also chairman of the town council. I'm declaring an emergency tomorrow, when news gets around that our sheriff-to-be was ambushed and killed. I'm appointing you as an emergency measure. By the time that we get around to an election, I'll take care of that little matter for you, too.'

'Any bonus jobs you'd like me to do before supper?'

'No.'

Cash's blue eyes stayed on Whitey, a faint grin on his lips.

'Oh,' said Whitey. 'Need money?'

'I don't need it. Just like a little binder on our agreement.'

Whitey opened a desk drawer. 'Say I give you a month's salary in advance. The town will pay you its wages through the council.' He handed Cash the money. 'Go out the back door.'

Cash put the bills in a tight hip pocket. 'Thanks. You pay the right price and you'll get anything you want out of me.' He turned and left the room, giving Duke a mocking nod as he passed him.

When the door was shut, Duke mumbled, 'I don't trust him. I never did like that smart-alecky kind.'

'He isn't a kind at all. He's the unique and only one of his brand that I've been able to find in the whole Southwest. No one likes or trusts him. That's just what I want. A man whose only star is money. That's why I sent you and Ben clear to Tucson to get him. If you and Ben and the others hate him it'll show, and the good citizens of Yellowrock won't figure he's our associate.'

'But you'll be appointin' him. Naturally they'll figure –'

'I won't mention his name. It will be brought up at the council by Hap Borland. Hap doesn't want me to press payment of his gambling debts. He'll be glad to keep quiet about it.'

'That's smart.' Duke swiped his gun out of its holster smoothly and twirled the cylinder with loving fingers. 'But in a showdown, I wouldn't count none on his gunplay. The gunslingers he's downed were all third rate. In a real match he'd be dead before he could get them slippery pearl handles to clear leather.'

'If I need any genuine shooting done, you're my man.'

Whitey circled the desk and slapped Duke lightly on the shoulder. 'Hell, Duke. That one isn't making three hundred a month on the strength of his gunning ability. He's making it because he's the most complete outcast in the territory. One of these days, when he's of no more use to us, you and Ben can play a hand of stud to see whether you get to shoot him or Ben gets to tear his head off his neck.'

*

17

When Cash left Whitey's office, he made his way toward the back door of the Alamo. Ben was seated where they'd left him, with two dancehall girls now in giggling conversation with him. They seemed to have cheered him up, for his heavy face was crinkled in a wide, ugly grin. He saw Cash and the grin turned into a toothy hostile stare. He leaned forward and whispered something to the girls. They glanced up at Cash and laughed hysterically.

Cash pushed through the swinging doors and stepped out onto the hard-packed earth of the alley. He moved casually to the street, then walked along the wide boardwalk, taking in the town. The lamps of the Longbranch flooded light into the store window next to it. There, under a card saying *Clymer's Dry Goods Emporium – Special from New York*, was a red gingham dress. He looked at it and shook his head. After twenty years red gingham was still in style. But he didn't want to think about that.

Around the corner from the El Dorado he found a restaurant. He went in.

Two hardrock prospectors down on their luck were hunched over plates of beans in one corner. A cowboy in a homespun shirt and slouch hat, with no heels on his boots to speak of, sat near them staring at a cup of coffee. Half a dozen skinned rabbits hung at one end of the wall facing him. Ma Bracken, a heavy, red-faced woman with muscles that showed through the fat on her arms, leaned one plump hand on his table and put the other on an ample hip. 'We got frijoles and beans.'

'That all you got?'

'I can make you a beefsteak, but it'll cost you a dollar.'

'Okay, but make sure it's dead.'

After eating, he walked back along Front Street to the Holiday Hotel, the only three-storey building in town. The gray-haired night clerk read his signature upside down across the desk and said, 'All right, Mr. Jefferson. Your bags were delivered by the stage line. We've arranged to have you in Room Twenty-three if that's satisfactory.' He handed Cash the key.

Lying in the dark of his room, Cash remembered Whitey's slick rundown of his life, and that reminded him of the red gingham dress.

18

'Family killed in a Confederate raid,' Whitey had said. But the way he'd said it showed he had no idea of what he was saying.

Before the soldiers had come to their isolated farm that night, the Jeffersons hadn't even known the war had begun.

His mother had said, 'Bruce, come look at Sally's new dress.'

It was red gingham. Mother had worked on it for three weeks. While his father puffed dreamily at a pipe, Sally had asked merrily, 'Well, little brother, how do you like it?'

There was the thunder of rifles outside, and a window near him bent inward before tumbling down in a tinkling cascade. A voice outside shouted, 'It's only a farmhouse!' and someone answered, 'They're Northerners. That's all that counts!'

The Rebs had set a haywagon on fire and rolled it down across the front yard to smash against the house. One corner of the wagon had slammed through a large window, throwing blazing hay into the living room. The impact had knocked a china cabinet down, and the edge of it hit Cash on the forehead. That was the last he remembered until he woke up with orange flames eating swiftly into the woodwork around him. He got to a window that was blackening with the heat, and smashed it with his hand. Outside, he fainted.

The bodies of his sister, mother, and father had been found later inside the house. Neighbors figured the girl's gingham dress had caught fire from the burning hay. Before the mother and father could put out those flames, they had themselves been caught in the blazing fire that swept quickly through the house. . . .

'Lived with an uncle,' Whitey had said.

Uncle Dave Wharton's own son had died of pneumonia after Dave had lashed the skin off the boy's back and sent him dressed in paper-thin moccasins and worn, hand-me-down shirt and pants to find a stray calf in a winter storm.

The time had come when Cash knew he would die too if he didn't get away from the merciless beatings and the killing work.

'Went to Texas,' Whitey had said. 'Was a brush popper.'

19

Cash had spent two years popping the brush, the toughest way to make a living ever invented. Riding hell-bent for leather through tall, jungle-thick scrub oak and cactus and every mean, sharp, tearing kind of tree and brush there is, and if you're lucky you catch a scrawny, wild pony every now and then that will bring at most twenty dollars on the market. He'd teamed with another youngster, a half-breed Comanche who was willing to live a hard life in order to be independent. The two of them had lived with the Comanches one year. Then, when they'd had a good summer, capturing five wild-eyed mustangs, his partner had tried to kill him. He'd stabbed Cash rather than waste a bullet, and left him for dead. Cash had found him later in a Fort Worth bar. And that had been the first time he'd killed a man.

A well-heeled Texan had liked the way Cash handled his old, single-action Navy Colt and had offered him five hundred dollars to repeat the performance on a personal enemy he had in San Antonio. Cash had accepted, and in one thundering split second had earned more than he would have made in two years of brush popping. The judge had ruled self-defense.

About that time the name 'Bruce' had disappeared and he'd been tagged with the nickname 'Cash'. Good whisky, good clothes, high living, and no friends. No loyalties or love to drain his strength; nothing but excitement and sheer meanness to hold him together. That was the best life.

In the morning Cash was awakened by a well-dressed young man who tapped sharply, like an uncertain wood-pecker, at his door. 'My name's Grayson,' he said. 'I'm secretary of the town council of Yellowrock. They called a meeting early this morning, because of – a certain incident. They wonder if you'd be able to come over with me.'

'Sure. Soon as I pull on my boots.'

The meeting was being held in an empty loft above Borland's General Store. Whitey Hall was seated at the head of a long plank table surrounded by a dozen men who looked up as Cash came through the door.

'This is Mr. Jefferson,' Grayson said.

'Come in, come in,' Whitey Hall said in a cold businesslike way. 'Sit down. Mr. Borland here has been saying some nice things about you, Mr. Jefferson.' He gestured to a stout, balding man at his left. 'You remember Mr. Borland?'

Cash said cautiously, 'I seem to recall the face.'

'Well, he remembers you. He was living in El Paso while you were deputy sheriff there. He informs us that you handled yourself well. Very well.'

'Oh.'

'I'll come right down to cases, Jefferson. This council arranged to hire a sheriff. He was killed yesterday on his way to town; no one knows why or who did it, but I've seen fit to declare an emergency. Things have come to a sorry pass when you can't even get a sheriff into town alive. Borland told us this morning that he'd seen you in town last night and suggested to us that, if you're willing, we put you on the payroll in the other man's place. The pay is one-fifty a month.' Hall's face set into serious lines. 'However, it's only fair to warn you now that the job won't be an easy one. You'll have to ride roughshod over hell-raisers and troublemakers and outright lawbreakers in this town to tame it down. If you have no prior commitments, I think I can speak for all of us in saying that the town needs you.'

'I was just passing through on my way north. I didn't have any definite plans.'

'Then you'll take the job?'

'Mr. Jefferson,' a stern, hook-nosed man interrupted, 'have you done any law enforcing except in El Paso?'

'No,' Cash replied, afraid to go out on a limb.

'Seems to me,' another said, 'that I heard somewhere about a Jefferson that shot a man in a bar down near the border. San Antone, if I recollect right. That you?'

'Yes, it was. A man makes enemies when he's trying to do the job right.'

Whitey commented, 'I think we can count ourselves fortunate that a man like Mr. Jefferson is in town and free to accept our offer at a time like this.' He turned to Cash. 'Will you take the job?'

'Maybe he'd like some time to think it over,' someone suggested.

'That won't be necessary,' Cash told them. 'I'd like to have a crack at the job.'

'Done.' Hall reached for a leather bag near him. 'We have copies of the usual papers to sign.' He turned to the second man on his left. 'What about the badge of office, Brockwell?'

Brockwell said, 'We asked Sullivan about that when we wrote last time. He said we didn't need to get a badge for him. He had one. He wore it in all those towns he'd worked in. So we didn't get one. And somebody either stole Sullivan's or they're burying it with him right now.'

Cash finished signing the papers before him and said, 'There's no need to have one right away. I can get along without it for the time being.'

Hall took the papers and put them in the bag. 'Yellowrock's a growing town. Being its first sheriff will probably present some problems, but I'm sure you'll overcome them. Would you like to meet me at the new jail in, say, fifteen minutes? It's almost finished, but perhaps you can suggest some improvements.'

'Fine.'

The others wished him good luck and he thanked them. Out on the street, he headed for the nearest bar and downed three quick shots.

'You're drinkin' like you just came off the great desert,' the bartender commented.

'Yeah?' Cash lifted two more and paid the man. Then he walked out and looked up and down the street. Walking south, he at last saw the skeleton of a building on Allen Street. He stood in front of it and waited for Hall. After a few minutes he began to inspect the structure.

After twenty minutes Ben came striding down the street, his small eyes angry in his huge, square face.

'This is one lousy jail,' Cash said as the big man came up to him. 'Where's Whitey?'

'This ain't the jail! This is the damned church! Whitey sent me to find you.'

The jail was set back on Corral Street on the next block. It was separated from the church by a two-storey stable which made it impossible to see one from the other.

Ben left Cash before they got to Whitey, who stood near

the jailhouse. It was much nearer completion than the church, its walls half sided, its roof shingled.

'I didn't like the way the council hesitated about hiring you,' Whitey said. 'I figured they'd jump at the chance. Wonder if any of them suspect you're my man? I don't want you tied up with me in any way.'

'Naturally I'm tied up with you. You're chairman of the council. The council's my boss.'

'Who knows you came into town with Duke and Ben?'

'Plenty of people.'

'Who?'

'Stage drivers.'

'They're mine. I own the line.'

'Couple of girls were talking with Ben when I left your office last night. They saw me.'

'They're mine. No trouble.'

Cash shook his head. 'Is there anything around here you don't own?'

'Anyone else see you?'

'Just a kid and an old man who were on the stage.'

'I didn't know anything about a kid.'

'He got on at Bancroft. Guess they dropped him off before we got to Yellowrock.'

'You guess? Don't you know?'

'I was asleep.'

Whitey frowned. 'The old man I know about; he's a fool preacher. I'll tie a can to his tail like I did the last gospel spieler. No trouble. But the kid I don't know about. I don't like the idea of him shooting his mouth off about how you and Duke and Ben were all on that coach together.'

'It's no crime that I happened to come into town with your two stooges. It could happen to any unfortunate traveler.'

'How come the kid was up to Bancroft in the first place?'

'He rode up there and back after he found the sheriff.'

'He found Sullivan?' Whitey's hard, flinty eyes narrowed. 'And neither you or Duke bothered to tell me! I'm surrounded by idiots!'

'What's the difference who found him?'

23

'My plan was for the stage drivers to find him. If the kid came along soon enough, Sullivan may have still been alive. He could have known I was in Yellowrock. He might have told the kid anything!'

'That's a big string of if's to worry about.'

Whitey stared blankly down the street, his jaw muscles twitching under the scar. 'The kid must live around Spangle Valley. Find out who he is.'

'Anything to satisfy your curiosity.'

Whitey ignored him. 'I guess you're about to make your first bonus.'

Cash grinned. 'Good.'

'Earning it will be a cinch. Find the kid. Make it look like a hunter did it. Kill him.'

CHAPTER THREE

Whitey stopped off at his stage office and learned through his superintendent that the driver had dropped the boy off about a mile beyond Buffaloback.

An hour later, well set up on a big buckskin quarter horse he'd picked out at the stable, Cash rode out of Yellowrock at an easy lope.

By the time his horse was stepping on its own shadow, Cash estimated Buffaloback to be a mile away. Far down in the sloping valley to his right he could see a winding line of trees and willows that marked the route of a river. He rode to it and gave his buckskin enough rein to drink. Crossing his leg over the pommel of the saddle, he pushed his hat back and stared at the water moving by. Maybe Whitey was right. Maybe the kid did have to be killed. But on the face of it, it seemed a little silly. Sullivan was probably dead before his foot left stirrup. Yet if the kid could expose Whitey, it would be a damned shame. Cash would lose the best-paying job he'd ever had.

When the buckskin began nosing the creekbank for a nibble of grass, Cash pulled his head up and pushed him into a splashing walk across the shallow stream. Sometime later he saw smoke lazing into the clear blue sky from the southeast. The thin line of smoke could be a camper, or it could the kid's home. He pointed the buckskin's nose toward it.

From the crest of the second rolling hill between him and the smoke, he saw a cabin set in a clearing in the draw below. Behind and to one side of the cabin was a barn. As Cash watched, a small figure came out of the barn and walked toward the house. Cash squinted. It was the boy he'd seen on the coach. He pulled his rifle from the saddle holster. An easy shot. No chance of just hurting the kid bad without killing him. But would it look like an accident? Anyone inside the cabin would know from the sound of the shot that it was fired close, in sight of the house.

Better to wait. Sooner or later the kid would take a walk.

Then would be the time. The youngster disappeared into the cabin.

Cash squeezed his mount into a careful, slow walk to a natural cove of trees a hundred yards closer to the cabin. He would be invisible here and could wait patiently. In a few minutes a taller, slender figure with long, bright red hair emerged from the cabin. It was a woman dressed in a man's pants and a plain flannel shirt. She crossed the small wooden porch and started walking toward where Cash was hidden.

Only a hundred feet away from his hiding place, she stopped and picked up a stick. She jabbed it into the grass near her feet, and there was a muted clang as the steel jaws of a small trap were sprung on the stick. A moment later she had untied the trap's thin holding chain from a nearby stump. Standing with the trap and chain in her hands, she turned toward the cabin and studied the ground around it, evidently looking for a better place to set the trap.

Cash saw a movement behind her, and a weaving, triangular head supported on a body as thick as a man's wrist appeared above the grass. The head stopped its sideways movement and hunched back, and Cash knew the diamondback was coiled, ready to strike. He could hear no warning rattle, but the woman should be able to hear it. What was the matter with her?

He was almost surprised to discover his rifle in his hands. He released the safety, swiftly pinpointed the still, crouched head in his sights, and squeezed the trigger.

The earth suddenly fell out from under him. His head was struck a blinding blow, and he passed out.

When Cash opened his eyes, a little boy was staring solemnly down at him. The boy said, 'You hit your head.'

Cash groped for memory, but it came hard. First the boy's face reminded him of his assignment. The cabin he was in would be the boy's home. Then, after a long mental search, he remembered the woman.

'Does your head feel bad?' the boy asked.

'Yeah. Terrible.' Cash started to sit up in the bunk he was lying on, but his head felt as if it were filled with large

26

rocks. The top was a mass of tight pain.

The woman came to the door and said, 'Hank, get some more water.'

She came to the bunk as the boy started to go for water. 'You'll be all right,' she said. 'What were you doing up on the hill?'

'I was just riding down toward the place here.'

'Why?'

'Just for the hell of it,' mumbled Cash.

'I didn't hear you coming.'

Cash suddenly remembered the diamondback. 'You must be deaf. From the size of that snake it must have had ten rattles, and you didn't hear it right behind you.' He groaned as she replaced a cloth wrapped around his head with a fresh, cold one. 'What happneed to me?'

'I'm not deaf. I didn't hear the snake because my son had a brush with him this spring. He found it in the wood-pile and chopped the rattle off – but the snake got away. That still doesn't explain why I didn't hear you.'

'I ride a quiet horse.'

'You don't know anything about that horse, or you wouldn't have shot from his back. He reared and slammed your head against a tree branch.'

Cash closed his eyes. 'The buckskin's gun shy, I know. But I didn't have time to worry about that.'

'Well – ' The feminine voice faltered and Cash looked up to see the faintest suggestion of tears in her eyes. 'I suppose I'd better thank you. It must have started to strike just as you shot. The – rattler brushed against my ankle.'

Really looking at her for the first time, Cash realized that she was quite beautiful. Her large green eyes filled as she finished talking, and she left the cabin.

When Hank came in carrying a bucket of water, Cash ignored the throbbing in his head and sat up in the bunk.

The boy said, 'I took care of your horse. Ma'll be back in a minute.' He explained in a whisper, 'She's out on the porch gettin' back to normal. She's scared somethin' terrible of snakes.'

Cash said, 'You're the kid who found Sullivan, aren't you?'

Hank dropped his eyes. 'Yes.'

'You talk to him?'

'Some.'

'What about?'

The boy raised his eyes to meet Cash's levelly. He said after some thought, 'I ain't sure if that's your affair, mister.'

'Maybe you're right. But could you tell me this? Was any of the talk about anybody in Yellowrock?'

'No.'

'Okay. Thanks, kid.'

The boy's mother came through the door. She said, 'I'd still be interested to know what brought you here. Hank recognized you. You rode on the stage with him yesterday. He tells me you're a gunman.'

Cash stood up, and suddenly realized his guns were gone, 'I am. I'm Yellowrock's new sheriff.'

'You are?' She smiled slowly and with warmth. 'I'm happy to hear that. We've needed a sheriff for so long. After what happened yesterday I was afraid we never would get one in Yellowrock.'

Cash rubbed his head gently. 'I'm so new that I haven't got a badge yet. But I wanted to come out to thank your son for what he did yesterday.'

Hank looked embarrassed and pleased and somehow sad. 'That was nice of you, mister,' he mumbled.

'Get some wood for the fire, Hank.' The woman brushed her hair back and smiled at Cash again. 'You'll have to stay for dinner.' She pulled the cupboard curtain back and began exploring the shelves. 'I'm sorry for behaving the way I did. Living alone as we do, unexpected strangers can be frightening. Oh!' She turned and faced him again. 'We don't know each other's names. I'm Virginia Brendan.'

'My name's Jefferson. Cash Jefferson. And I'd hate to ride back into town and have it get around that on my first day in office a young woman disarmed me. Would you tell me where my guns are?'

The boy entered with the wood as Cash finished speaking.

Virginia Brendan called, 'Hank, you can get Mr. Jefferson's guns now.'

The boy came back shortly, leaning against the weight of the two revolvers on the black leather belt. 'Sure a fancy set,' he said almost reverently.

'They're okay for later on.' Cash buckled them around his waist and settled the holsters right. 'But for starting a fellow ought to have a rifle.'

'I got a percussion cap long gun,' Hank said. 'Only fault is I ain't got no ball or powder. And,' he added lamely, 'no percussion caps.'

'Haven't got,' his mother corrected him, beginning to set the table. 'It must be quite exciting, Mr. Jefferson, coming to a new town to be its first sheriff. How do you go about it? What do you do first?'

'I guess that depends on the town, ma'am,' Cash said.

'I suppose your just being there is the most important thing.'

'Pardon?'

'I mean – if a man comes into town, regardless of what sort of person he is, he'll say to himself, "There's a sheriff in this town," and he'll mind his manners better than if he knew he could do whatever he wanted. Isn't that right?'

'Might be. But there are a lot of men who are inclined the other way and don't give a good – a hoot whether the whole United States Army is in town.'

'Yes. I'm afraid so.' She glanced at him seriously as she worked. 'There are a lot like that in Yellowrock.'

'So I've been told.'

During dinner Cash found conversation progressively harder. Hank's mother seemed troubled. The boy kept the talk going with quiet, intense questions about the outside world, where Cash had been and what he had done. Finally, wanting to hear the sound of her voice, Cash asked her, 'What did you have that trap set for on the hill?'

'Coyote. We've got a few chickens out behind the barn. He's been trying to get at them.'

'Why don't you try behind that line of elderberries running up close to the barn? Coyotes like to stay hid, even at night.'

'I'll try that spot,' she said, and lapsed into silence.

When Cash finished his coffee, he told her, 'That was a fine dinner, ma'am, and I'm much obliged. I've got to get started back now.'

Hank said, 'I'll bring your horse down from the stable,' and hurried out of the room.

29

'Mr. Jefferson.' The green eyes held his own intently as she spoke. 'It has occurred to me, especially after what happened to that man Sullivan, that one of the first things a sheriff in a town like Yellowrock might possibly do would be to get himself shot.'

'That's a likelihood.'

'Or, on the contrary, to shoot first.'

'That's considered preferable.'

'I'm quite serious. It must be hard, and lonely, sometimes.'

'Well.' Cash frowned uneasily at the table. 'The pay's good.'

'Nothing can pay for some things. You know that as well as I do.'

'What do you and your boy do here on this place?'

She leaned to one side and gestured out the window to where the draw opened out into wide, rolling pasture. 'These days I work at Clymer's Dry Goods Emporium in Yellowrock three days a week. But thirty-five hundred acres out there is mine. If I can get enough money together I'd like to buy a few head of cattle, hire a man to help me, and start a small ranch.'

Cash grinned as they stood up from the table. 'If I'm in the market for some dry goods I'll get them at Clymer's.'

'What I meant to say before,' she said, smiling, 'is that Yellowrock is a wild, thoroughly mean town. If you feel like talking to someone, like getting away from everything for a little while, please feel free to call on us. Hank and I would both be happy to see you.'

'Thanks very much, Mrs. Brendan. I'll do that.' Cash returned her smile and went out to the porch, putting his hat on gingerly.

'You'll have to lift your saddle up,' Hank said, tying the buckskin's reins to the hitching-post. 'I pulled it off all right, but I can't heave it back up.'

'Okay.' Cash took the saddle from the porch and tossed it over. He pulled the cinch tight, took the reins and swung into the saddle. Hank kept pace with the horse's slow walk for a short distance. Then he said, 'Mister?'

Cash stopped and looked down. 'Yeah?'

The boy hooked his fingers around one stirrup strap and

stared up, his face set in firm decision. 'Mister, my dad always said to do the best you could for folks who did anything for you. And I've been thinkin' about what you did for Ma. She would've died if that big rattler had hit her.'

'So?'

'Up until yesterday, the finest thing I owned was that rifle, and that ain't any good, really. Especially for a fellow who owns guns like yours.' Hank swallowed and reached his free hand into his pocket. 'But the best thing I've got now is this. And it's somethin' you said you ain't got.' He stretched his hand up and Cash saw the shiny outlines of a tin star in his fist. 'It's a real badge. Mr. Sullivan gave it to me.'

'How come?'

The boy lowered his eyes. 'He could see that I was – takin' it hard, him hit so bad and all. He was tryin' to smooth it over, make it easy on me cause I'm only a kid. I'd put my straw hat down to shade his eyes, and he said that was a mighty fine hat and he'd trade me his badge and his horse for it. Then, after a while, when he was sure the men who'd shot him wouldn't come back and hurt me, he – let himself die.'

'What happened to the horse?'

'She was a calico mare. She ran away. Maybe I'll be able to find her, yet. I'd like to have that man's horse.'

'Good luck. As for the badge, you don't owe me anything. Forget it.'

'I owe you more'n I got. I'd like for you to have it, mister.'

Cash took the badge, looked at it briefly and put it in his shirt pocket. 'Thanks, kid. Don't call me mister – the name's Cash.'

'I'm Hank.' He stood back and put his hands in his hip pockets.

Cash waved in a gesture of good-by and pushed his horse into a quick, thumping trot toward Yellowrock.

Late in the afternoon Cash left the buckskin at the Corral Street stable and walked through the long shadows to his hotel. He poured a basin full of water and washed. He was hanging the towel back on the rack when there was a knock at the door.

'Come in,' he called.

The door opened and one of the men he'd seen in Whitey Hall's office the night before stepped in. 'Hall wants to see you,' he said.

'Where is he?'

'The Alamo. He says for you to use the back door.'

'I'll be there. Tell him I'm washing up so I'll make a good impression on him.'

The man grunted and shut the door behind him.

At the rear entrance to the Alamo, Cash pushed through the swinging doors and walked to Whitey's private office. At his knock the door swung open and he stepped in. The man who had brought him the message held the knob. Whitey, seated at his desk, said, 'Go on out, Garf. We want to talk alone.'

As Garf went out, Cash said, 'For a gent who doesn't want to be tied up with me, you sure see me a lot.'

'Did you get the kid?'

'No. All I've shot all day is a rattlesnake. I don't suppose you pay a bounty on rattlesnakes?'

'Stop trying to be so damned funny.' Whitey's face was tight with fury. 'What happened? Why didn't you get that kid?'

'I'd have had to shoot everybody for twenty miles around. He'd already told a dozen people everything he knew.'

'What did he know? Was my name mentioned?'

'Nope. You're in the clear.'

Whitey breathed deeply and settled back in his chair.

Cash picked up the decanter on Hall's desk and poured a shot. 'You want one too?'

'Yes.' Whitey's color was coming back. He muttered, 'From what I know about you I'm surprised you didn't kill the boy anyway, so you could collect the bonus I promised you.'

Cash's hand hesitated pouring the second shot. Then he continued pouring. 'You know, Whitey, the truth is I didn't even think of that. What do you get paid around here for being honest?'

'I'd planned on five hundred for shooting the kid. Half

32

the usual price, because it's damn sure that a youngster like that ain't dangerous.'

'I'd feel bad to think I'd cheated myself out of five hundred dollars,' Cash mused.

'Tell you what. It's worth that for me to be sure I'm in the clear. You'll get it. I like my boys to be happy.'

'That makes this boy happy.'

There was a light tap at the door and Hall said, 'Yes?'

Duke came in followed by Ben, whose huge bulk nearly filled the door frame.

'Did you find out about Griggs?' Whitey asked.

'Yeah.' Duke handed him a folded piece of paper. 'Got word at the telegraph office just now that he's comin'. Be here in a couple days.'

'Matt Griggs?' Cash put his empty glass down and sat on Hall's desk.

'Yes,' said Whitey.

'What do you want with another gunslinger? Is Duke getting too old?'

Duke glanced at Cash. Whitey read the telegram, then said, 'You've got it all wrong. Every now and then one of my business competitors in Yellowrock makes a play for a little more power. Moss Hewitt owns the Alhambra and he's been doing fairly well. Now he's making his play to do better. He's importing Griggs.'

Cash nodded, 'So the new sheriff, realizing that Griggs is a longhorn desperado from way back, warns him to leave town. And when he refuses, shoots him.'

'Not quite,' Whitey said, and Duke's narrow eyes flicked triumphantly at Cash. 'Griggs will be Duke's meat.'

Duke said, 'Griggs would nail your hide to a wall in double time.'

'And you're so skinny he might miss you?' Cash suggested.

'Cut it out, both of you.' Hall stood up and began pacing the floor. 'There is one thing I want you to do, Cash. Tomorrow's payday at the mines. It'll be a big night. About nine o'clock I'll have a few boys spotted around the Alhambra. I want you to go in and start a legitimate ruckus. Arrest one of the dealers for using stacked cards – something like that. I want that place

33

wrecked – understand me? – not just dented, but demolished. And throw as many of the Alhambra men as you can round up into jail. It'll make you look good to the rest of the town. Then, when Griggs gets in the day after, I'll want you to be an eyewitness to the shooting.'

'Won't it look kind of funny for poor old Moss Hewitt at the Alhambra to have so much headache all at once, when you own five saloons? As a conscientious sheriff, chances are better than even it would be one of your joints I'd wreck.'

Whitey shrugged. 'Good point. Except that as far as most folks are concerned I own only the Alamo. I've got good men taking care of the other places for me.'

Ben spoke for the first time. 'Can I help to bust up that place, boss?'

'Drop around the Alhambra for a drink around nine tomorrow night. I don't see how it could be a first-class riot without you there,' Whitey told him.

'I'll be there. The place'll get the hell smashed out of it, even if our new sheriff chickens out. Duke tells me he ain't even got a badge yet to back up his big mouth.'

'Matter of fact, I have, Ben.' Cash took the star from his shirt pocket and tossed it lightly in the palm of his hand.

'Where'd you get it?' Whitey demanded. 'I didn't think there was one for two hundred miles around.'

'This one belonged to a fellow whose passing we all mourn. I guess fate just wanted me to have it, instead of him.

Whitey said softly, 'Sullivan's?'

'The very same.'

A large grin worked slowly across Whitey's face. Then he leaned his head back and roared with laughter. Ben smiled too, not understanding, and Duke said, 'Damn!' though his face didn't change.

When Whitey's laughter had run down, Duke said, 'Sullivan will be turnin' over in his grave.'

'Why, Duke,' Cash said quietly. 'He won't be turning over in his grave. He'll be lying at rest, downright pleased that his badge is bringing law and order to this town – even though someone else is wearing it.'

Whitey said, 'If a bullet hadn't finished him, this would. He'd die of plain shock.'

34

'Why don't you pin it on now?' Duke said to Cash. 'I'd like to see what a real, live lawman looks like.'

'I'll put it on in the morning. I've got a fancy red shirt it'll look good on. Got to break it in right.'

'How'd you come to lay hands on it?' Duke asked.

'Sullivan gave it to the kid. He gave it to me.'

'How much did the kid want for it?' Whitey asked.

'He gave it to me for nothing.'

'That's about what it's worth. When you put it on tomorrow, I want you to be a model lawman. Just remember to play sheriff with the right people and at the right time. And put the fear of God in them.'

Cash put the star back in his pocket and started for the door. 'Yeah. And I won't forget who's God, Whitey.'

CHAPTER FOUR

In the morning Cash started to put on a white shirt. Then he remembered his half-joking talk about the red shirt and out of stubbornness ruffled through his warbag until he found it. The star stood out brightly against the scarlet background.

Downstairs the little room clerk looked up and smiled, professionally pleasant. 'My, Mr. Jefferson. I heard you were made sheriff, and I see it's official now.'

'That's right.'

'I hope you'll be staying on with us here. It won't do us any harm.'

'What do you mean?'

'Why – I just mean that having the right people staying in a hotel tends to increase its good reputation and its popularity. You understand.'

'Oh. I hadn't thought of moving.'

'I'm happy to know that. Good morning, sir.'

Cash went out to the walk and stood for a moment letting the rays of the early sun beat warmly against his face. Half a dozen old-timers were seated in rockers on the front porch of the hotel. He could feel their eyes on his back. When he turned they were leaning forward in their chairs, watching him. As he started down the street he could hear their whispering voices behind him.

Two bearded miners in overalls stared impassively at him, quietly taking in the badge, his guns and his face. A middle-aged woman he'd never seen before beamed at him as she stepped from a nearby buggy and said, 'Good morning, Sheriff.' Two little boys stopped wrestling in the dusty street and sat up to stare at him with silent, intense curiosity as he passed.

Distinctly uncomfortable, Cash suddenly realized that the people on the other side of the street were stopping to look at him. He swung abruptly into the first restaurant he came to. It was breakfast time and the place was crowded. The door slammed shut behind him and the loud voices, the banging of dishes and the shuffling of feet stopped as though all the noise in the world had been turned off. Cash could hear his own breathing, and was painfully aware of a hundred faces turned toward him.

A thickset miner hurried in through the doorway behind Cash and brushed roughly against him. 'Get outa the way,' he grumbled. 'What the hell are you blockin' the – ' He saw the badge as he looked back at Cash. He hesitated. 'Excuse me.'

'No offense.'

Cash sat at a table, and the noise gradually worked back to somewhere near normal. . . .

On the street again, Cash decided to take the long way around to look over the jail. To his relief, once he got off Front Street he passed no one for three blocks. Near the corner of Allen, a block before Corral, a small man who seemed vaguely familiar approached him.

'What a pleasant surprise!' the man said.

'What is?'

'That Yellowrock has a sheriff. You and I rode in on the stage together. The day that other lawman was ambushed. My name's Williams.'

'Yes. I remember you now. I was a little drunk on that trip.'

'I know. You drank half the whisky between here and Tucson. You drink like that often?'

'Time and again.'

'Amazing. Could you go a mug of coffee?'

'Thanks for the offer, but I'm staying out of the main part of town.'

Williams looked keenly at Cash, searching for the thought behind his eyes. 'This your first day?'

'Yes, sort of.'

'And they're watching you so closely you're beginning to wonder what you look like.'

'You have that problem?'

'To a degree. My invitation for coffee was at my place just up the street. I've been doing some work on it.' Williams gestured toward the skeleton of a church and Cash saw that the old man had a remarkably hard, square jaw.

'Okay. I'll go a cup. My name's Cash Jefferson.' He recalled what Whitey had said about running the preacher out of town. Might not be as easy as Whitey thought.

Williams had a kerosene burner rigged up in the back of the church. Sunlight streamed through the open frame-work above. When he put a mug of coffee in front of Cash he said, 'As long as it doesn't rain, this building ought to be comfortable.'

'I wonder if you'll get more business here, or I'll get more behind the stable. That's where the jail is.'

Williams slapped sawdust from a plank with his hat and sat down with his coffee. 'It's not an equal contest. You can drag your customers in by the seat of their britches. I have to invite mine politely.'

Cash blew softly on the steam rising from his mug. 'The worst I can offer is hanging. You can threaten them with hell-fire.'

'I don't believe in threats. You know, we're actually in the same business, in a way.'

'I don't see how.'

Williams settled back against a supporting beam. 'You take mining or cowpunching or gambling, say, and the way I look at it a man in those jobs – or in most jobs – is mainly just pulling down his pay. Now you take a preacher or a sheriff or a teacher – they're helping other people. If you, Cash, put a thief in jail, you're not really doing it to punish him, but to protect the people he steals from. You're primarily helping people, instead of yourself. Which is what I hope I'm doing, in my own way. See?'

'That's an interesting notion, but I'm a self-helper from way back. Speaking of help, I wouldn't figure a preacher would have to do all the carpentry on his church.'

'I won't. I'm supposed to start getting volunteer workers tomorrow. I don't suppose you're so sorry about my sad fix that you'd like to hammer a few nails?'

'Not that sorry. I'll be pretty busy.' Cash put his mug down. 'But feel free to holler out over the stable if someone steals the collection plate.'

They stood up, and Williams said, 'It'll be interesting, since we're starting at the same time, to see if we do any good in our respective work. I hear there's a large, tough segment of the town that has no love for either of our offices.'

'I've heard that. Thanks for the coffee.'

'Any time.'

Cash found the jailhouse nearer completion. The exterior was finished and several workmen were busy inside. There were a desk and a chair in his office. He sat down and looked through the drawers of the first desk he'd ever had. They were all empty except the top middle drawer. It held ink, a pen, some paper, and a thick, worn book that someone had placed there titled General Information on Conduct and Behavior of Officers of The Law in New York City.

He put his feet on the desk and began thumbing through the volume.

In the early evening Cash's hunger finally overcame his reluctance to go out on the street wearing the badge. He had a leisurely dinner at the Golden Steer and was slightly surprised when he saw that it was eight forty-five – time to start for the Alhambra.

The town was seething with movement and life. Bars and saloons were filled to capacity and an overflow of boisterous men filled the doorways and spilled out into the streets. The men shouted or talked together loudly, while those who'd got an early start on their liquor burst into snatches of wild, profane song as they went from one saloon to the next. Surrounded by a group of laughing miners, one bearded old man kicked up his boots as he did a short, spirited dance in the middle of the street. Somewhere in town revolver blasts rocked the already turbulent air.

In the noisy turmoil only a few people noticed Cash. Those who did spot his badge showed irritated respect as they moved sullenly aside to give him room to pass along the walk.

The Alhambra was a big bar and gambling house, like any of a thousand others Cash had seen. The bar ran straight to the back of the room from the entrance. To the right were about three dozen tables, mostly faro and black-jack. Two large roulette wheels were set up near the far wall.

Cash eased into the bar and ordered whisky. The bar-keep took in his badge with a swift glance and reached for a bottle, just as a large man wearing a green eye shade shouldered roughly up to the counter and yelled, 'Louis! Give me a quick one.'

The bartender ignored him. Pouring a shot with a professional twist of the wrist, he shoved the glass to Cash.

'I'll trouble you for that.' The big man's fist went around the glass. 'What's the matter with you, Louis? Serving a saddlebum when I'm thirsty and have to get back to my table?'

The bartender said, 'You ought to take a better look at him.'

The man swung around and stared at Cash. He saw the star and smiled sarcastically. 'Now ain't that sweet? So you're the law in Yellowrock!' He raised his voice so the men around him could hear. 'Look what we got ourselves here. A real, honest-to-goodness sheriff, dressed up in a pretty red shirt. Ain't he a darlin'?'

'I'll take my drink now,' Cash said. 'I'd be obliged if you'd put it back on the bar and take your hands off it.'

'Maybe you didn't hear me. I'm thirsty.' The man raised the glass to his lips.

'You're making this easy.' Before the gambler could tilt the glass, the barrel of Cash's Colt slammed into the side of his head and he fell backward, knocking a man behind him off balance.

Two house men saw the commotion and plowed through the room toward Cash. He buffaloed one of them with the gun in his hand and knocked the other over the bar with a left that started from the sawdust-covered floor.

The riot was on.

Someone smashed the heavy chandelier hanging in the centre of the room with a well-aimed chair. A bottle sailed across the room and shattered the huge mirror behind the bar. A cowpuncher at a faro table scooped a pile of silver dollars into his hat and dived out the nearest window without bothering to open it.

Out of the side of his eye Cash saw Ben up-end a roulette table. As it crashed to the floor, the huge man surged through the battling masses, scattering them right and left, and headed for the piano standing on a built-up platform in the corner. The little pianist was hunched over the key-

40

board, his fingers flying as he tried the impossible task of calming the rioters with music.

Ben squeezed between the piano and the wall and shoved. The piano curved out off the platform and thundered to the floor, smashing one of the pianist's legs under it. Ben laughed loudly at the squirming of the trapped man.

Cash ducked a swinging brass spittoon and brought his knee up into the stomach of his attacker. He saw Ben circling the piano toward the little man under it, a table leg gripped in his hands like a club. Cash battled his way through the raging fighters and caught Ben's shoulder. 'Leave him alone.'

Ben shoved away the restraining arm. 'What for? I don't like piano plunkers.'

'There's no need for killing. This riot's going to stay legal. Get out.'

Ben snarled like a great animal and started for Cash. Cash flipped his Colt to a level with Ben's chest. 'I said get out.'

The big man paused, then spun around and crashed away through the crowd toward the door, scattering men before him with his powerful, flailing arms. He fell once. The prone man who had accidentally tripped him had struggled to all fours when Ben stood back up and stomped down with his boot. The man's arm was ripped by Ben's spur and the bone snapped under the weight of the boot. Cash could hear his scream of pain. Then Ben was gone.

The riot lasted fifteen minutes, and when the crowd had scrambled out the door the place was a shambles. About eight or ten men were hurt too much to move, or unconscious. The pianist had passed out from pain. Cash's shirt was ripped, but he was unhurt. He walked slowly about the room, examining the wreckage. As he went by the piano the man pinned beneath it groaned and started to move feebly. He opened his eyes and said through clenched teeth, 'Can you get that off my leg?'

Cash tried to lift the piano, but it was too heavy. He took the table leg Ben had dropped near the man, and, using it as a lever, raised the piano enough for the man to pull his foot free.

'Thanks, Sheriff,' the pianist gasped.

'You're smashed up pretty bad. Better take it easy.' Cash helped him into a chair that had escaped being broken.

At a rustling sound behind him, Cash whirled and whipped out his gun. The bartender was standing up behind his bar, a pick handle in his hands. He leaned it quietly back under the counter.

'How come you didn't make some use of that in the fracas?' Cash asked him.

'If a fight is controllable I come out swinging it.' The bartender shrugged. 'Otherwise I settle down under the mahogany and wait it out.'

'If there's a bottle left in one piece back there, I'll take that drink now.'

In addition to the men that Cash had downed in the beginning there was one other Alhambra employee stretched out on the floor, the big man who had grabbed his drink. Cash disarmed them as they came to and herded them to the bar. He finished his whisky and took the four men to jail. Along the street noisy groups of men became silent, staring in astonishment at the procession.

He put all four of them in the same cell and locked it.

'Hey, fellow,' one of them whined, gingerly feeling a large swelling behind his ear. 'Why are you pickin' on us?'

'You were disturbing the peace.' Cash went back to the front office and sat down. He twirled the keys aimlessly before dropping them on the desk. He was tired and wanted to go to his room at the hotel, but he couldn't decide whether to walk away and leave his jail or not. 'Hell,' he complained to himself, 'you make someone a prisoner and he turns right around and takes away your own freedom.'

At around ten o'clock the office door swung open and a short, dark man came in. 'I'm Moss Hewitt,' he said. 'Own the Alhambra. I was out of town. What happened?'

'You missed a little excitement.'

Hewitt took a large handkerchief from a hip pocket and mopped his face. 'My place is ruined. It'll cost me a fortune to put it back in shape.'

'I wouldn't worry too much about fixing things up. In your shoes I'd be thinking about setting up shop somewhere else.'

42

'What d'you mean?' Hewitt looked at Cash sharply. 'You being paid off by someone who wants whole hog?'

'Dishonest gambling is contrary to the law. Two of your dealers had card mirrors hooked under their fingernails, and I ran across several shaved decks. Seems to me you weren't giving your clients an even shake, Moss.'

'The house has to have an edge.' Hewitt turned his palms up in worried innocence. 'You know we've all got our little tricks. But why the Alhambra? Why me? I heard my boys didn't treat you right. Okay, they're fired.' He lowered his voice to a whisper. 'Also, just for friendship, I could slip you maybe a hundred a month – just to be friendly.'

'That's nice of you, and I have a soft spot in my heart for hundred-a-month friendships. But the answer has to be no.'

'You're in the driver's seat now,' Hewitt said angrily. 'But you never know what tomorrow will bring. Maybe tomorrow you'll be out of the driver's seat. Maybe tomorrow you'll be in a coffin.'

'You anxious to join the boys in the back?'

Hewitt opened his mouth, shut it, then changed the subject. 'What's their bail?'

'No bail. I'll toss them out of here tomorrow. I'll do it early, while I'm still in the driver's seat.'

Hewitt went out angrily, and Cash stretched. He stood up and crossed the room to stand leaning against the door frame, watching thoughtfully down the dark, quiet street toward the still rambunctious main drag.

The sound of footsteps straightened him up, his hands slipping automatically to the butts of his revolvers. Two men walked into the light thrown through the jail window and one of them said, 'I see you're getting the feel of your job already.'

They stepped into his office. The man who had spoken was the young member of the city council named Grayson. He introduced the older man with him as Clem Clymer. 'We thought we'd drop over and congratulate you on getting a good start in bringing the law to town,' Grayson told him. 'You did fine to crack down on the Alhambra. And you certainly did a complete job. That was one of the meanest dives in town.'

Clymer, a square-faced old man with a handlebar

mustache, nodded his head briefly. 'Appears to me the whole town's a little bit tamer since that ruckus. You know this is the first time anybody's ever been arrested around here? And four of them at one crack – that's some beginning. We're downright glad to have you for our sheriff.'

Cash hid his embarrassment behind a curt word of thanks and said, 'A lady named Brendan work for you?'

'Sure does. Since her husband got killed by Indians a couple of years back. You know her?'

'Met her yesterday.'

'Virginia's like my own daughter. She's educated, and smart besides. And she's the prettiest female in the whole territory. Works three days, Thursday through Saturday, at my store. Business really booms when she's there. Every young buck for fifty miles thinks up some little thing to buy and comes in. That goes for Bill Grayson here, too.'

Grayson grinned. 'I've been asking her to marry me every Thursday for a year. No luck so far.'

'You're not planning on staying here in the jail all night, are you?' Clymer asked Cash.

'I was sort of wondering how far I ought to go playing nursemaid to the men in the back.'

'To hell with 'em,' Clymer said. 'They'll keep till morning. We'll walk you uptown a ways.'

Cash checked the cell once more, then locked the front door of the office and they walked slowly up the street.

Clymer said, 'I'm surprised that Whitey Hall didn't make more of a kick about the council making you sheriff.'

'Why?'

'I've always had him pegged for having more irons in the fire than a convention of drunk cattle rustlers.'

'Guess he feels he needs protection.'

'He's got it. He's always surrounded by two toughs. Fellows named Duke and Ben. And some others spend more time at the Alamo than necessary to get relief from the heat.'

'Hall is all right,' Grayson said. 'He's made more money out of Yellowrock than most of us, so he's got a right to look out for himself. But when it comes right down to cases he does fine by the town. He didn't balk at Jefferson's appointment. He also gave more than half the money to build the jail.'

'I've gotten along with him so far,' Cash said.

Clymer blew cigar smoke thoughtfully. 'If the time ever comes when you don't, keep your eyes about you. This town can't afford to lose a good sheriff.'

Cash left them at the corner of Allen and Front and continued on to the Holiday Hotel.

He stepped into his room and put a match to the kerosene lamp. Before he took off his torn shirt, Cash unpinned the badge. He blew on it sharply and shined it a little on his sleeve before putting it on top of the dresser.

He was up at six. The people he passed on his way to the jail still watched him, but their attention was more relaxed, less avidly curious. Half a dozen people spoke to him while several others nodded and a few glowered at him.

At the jail he sorted through the keys on his ring and opened the cell where the four men lay. The big man hurried out before the others. 'Next time it may be different,' he muttered.

'There won't be a next time for you. You're leaving town. You other three can do what you want – but keep out of trouble.'

'How long you giving me to get out of town?' the big gambler sneered.

'No hurry. Take all the time you want, but get out sometime before noon.'

A few minutes later one of the trio of gunmen Cash had seen at Whitey's office came in. 'My name's Saul. Whitey says you should know that Matt Griggs will be on the eleven o'clock stage.'

'Yes. I'm supposed to be there to pick up the pieces. Whose pieces they'll be I'm not sure.'

Saul grinned and said, 'No question in my mind. You ever see Duke shoot?'

'Haven't had the pleasure.'

'That's the only thing in this world that Duke is built for.' Saul closed the door behind him so he couldn't be overheard and Cash saw that he was younger than he looked at a casual glance. Now, talking about Duke, his features were almost boyishly enthusiastic. 'I seen him draw twice, and the thing is you don't even see it. He's got wrist

45

action. That's what does it. He uses his wrists a lot and his elbows only a little and his gunplay isn't just pro – it's magic.'

'That's fine. He sounds like just the man to run for President.'

'You'll see when he tackles Griggs. It'll be quite a show. Duke always likes to make a show of a shooting. Likes to lead up to it slowly, to make the other fellow nervous.'

'I'll bet he's a real circus.' Cash studied the young man. 'What are you tied up with those other two for? You don't seem to be their calibre.'

Saul frowned. 'You insultin' me?'

'No. I'm allowing you the bigger calibre.'

'Well, I tail with them, that's all. Garf, the one with the mustache, is my brother. Sometimes we don't get along. I get fed up. Fact is, every now and then I get the hankerin' to go up north to Wyoming country and set up a little place of my own. But Garf don't see it.'

'Do it yourself. Can't be a little brother all your life.'

'I ain't!' Saul threw his head up angrily. 'Things just ain't been right for it so far. Some day I'll do it.'

Cash shrugged. 'No matter to me. I was only curious why you tagged with them. Now I've got things to do, so beat it.'

'Okay. You'll see what I mean about Duke.'

Shortly after Saul disappeared through the door, Cash left the jail and went to the stable across the road where his buckskin quarter horse was boarded. An old stable buck put the horse's furniture on and Cash rode far out of town to a lonely spot.

Getting off, he roped the animal firmly to a tree and walked twenty feet away. He pulled a gun and shot twice into the air.

The buckskin whinnied in shrill terror and reared frantically against the rope. Cash sat on a rock and waited patiently a few minutes, then let loose with the Colt again. The horse trembled and rolled its eyes, but this time it didn't try to yank away from the tree.

Two hours and twenty shots later, Cash had worked his way up to the the restless but braver pony to do his shooting. He untied the rope from the tree and swung into the saddle. Trotting the buckskin to a wide clearing, he fired over its head. It pitched forward a little, breaking its stride, and flattened its ears, but gave him no serious trouble. He squeezed the horse into a run and fired twice more. On the last shot the galloping buckskin didn't shy its head away at all.

'Now,' Cash told it, drawing back to a trot, 'let's not try to break my head again.'

In town, Cash dropped the buckskin off at the stable and had breakfast. He was pleased to note that he was getting so he could hold his own against a room of staring eyes. Consequently, the eyes didn't stare so much.

The waiter made a big thing of serving him and when Cash paid his bill said, 'Hope everything was all right Sheriff. Always a pleasure to have you here.'

Cash had a drink at a bar across the street from the stage office. Through the window he watched for the stage to arrive. At ten to eleven the big gambler he'd told to leave town went into the office, carrying a bag. Cash could see him going through the motions of buying passage. 'I'll be damned,' Cash muttered. The gambler was actually leaving town before noon, on nothing more than Cash's word. It was an overwhelming compliment.

Within a few minutes the Alhambra pianist limped up to the stage office on a rude crutch and bought a ticket too. Three or four others got in line to buy seats on the stage, while the usual crowd gathered before the office on the sidewalk to watch the morning coach roll in.

Shortly after eleven there was the growing drum of hoof-beats out of Cash's sight up the street and a loud harsh, 'Kee-yah!' from the driver as the coach rumbled through town. It whirled into Cash's vision and drew to a stop before the office amid a swirling cloud of dust. It was a crowded coach, with four men riding on top and the rear boot piled high with baggage. While the passengers were unloading and people leaving Yellowrock were filling up their places, a fresh team in harness was brought smartly up to replace the spent horses.

There was no mistaking Matt Griggs. Tall and unhurried, he was the last man off the stage. He moved slowly, as though every motion meant something.

47

Cash walked out to the street and leaned back against the wall of the saloon, waiting for Duke to make an appearance.

Duke didn't show up.

Moss Hewitt met Griggs as the stage pulled out. The two of them walked toward the Alhambra as the rest of the crowd broke up. They had entered the demolished saloon when Whitey and Ben came out of the Alamo and moved towards Cash.

'Howdy, Sheriff,' Whitey called from thirty feet away. The passersby glanced at Whitey as he called, and Cash couldn't help admiring Hall's showmanship. No one who looked up and saw Ben as the big man approached Cash would ever suspect that the two men were on the same payroll. Ben's eyes were filled with a hate that could never be pretended. When Whitey stood before Cash, he said in a lower tone, 'Griggs get in all right?'

Cash folded his arms. 'Yes, he did. And that Duke is sure the fastest man I ever saw. He was here and gone so fast I never did see him. And he blasted Griggs so quick that Griggs don't even know he got shot.'

'Duke'll be here, don't you worry,' Ben growled.

'Firing pin on Duke's gun looked a bit dull when he went over it a little while ago,' Whitey explained. 'He's filing it down to a good point now. The rumour's being put out that Duke and Griggs are personal enemies of long standing. Don't want people thinking there are purely commercial motives behind this killing. You wait here.'

'Okay. I've got nothing better to do.'

Whitey and Ben went on down the street and disappeared around a corner. Cash lounged back against the wall and waited.

Five minutes later Griggs and Moss Hewitt left the Alhambra and stood outside talking.

Without turning his head, Cash knew when Duke appeared at the far end of the street. Everyone in Cash's range of sight stopped and stared and quickly got out of the street. Matt Griggs and Moss Hewitt stopped talking and turned to look.

Cash swung his head around slowly. Duke was on the other side of Front Street, four hundred feet beyond Cash.

He stood without moving, hands at his sides. But even motionless there was a terrible, swift force about him that Cash felt rather than saw. He suddenly reminded Cash of the diamondback he'd shot, the diamondback who'd completed a full lunge with his head shot off, striking with a reflex action so powerful it worked even after death.

Griggs took two steps across the boards before the Alhambra and stood at the edge of the walk. Like Duke, he wore only one gun. It hung low on his hip, a thin cord of buckskin stretching around his leg and securing the bottom end of his holster. He stood at the edge of the walk for a few seconds, studying the street and the sinister figure of Duke. He held his hands away from his sides and flexed his fingers wide. He slowly opened and shut his hands twice, like a concert player about to begin an intricate selection. Then he took one step down to the dirt street and waited.

Now Whitey's top gunman moved slowly forward, and as he came closer Cash knew the reason why Duke took his time. He liked to kill. He wanted to string it out as much as he could. His hands were now stiff with tension, his lips frozen in a straight, tight smile, and his eyes were glittering with a sort of black joy. Cash could tell that Duke liked having an audience.

Griggs wasn't easy to scare. As Duke came slowly nearer, he waited imperturbably, his hand now wide open, fingers extended straight down, thumb cocked at an angle.

Duke stopped almost abreast of Cash. He called to Griggs in a voice so low that Cash almost missed it. 'Griggs. Are you afraid to do some walking?' He waited.

Griggs frowned suspiciously. Then his lips twisted into a tiny, sardonic grin and he moved cautiously forward.

Cash could hear his own heart pounding as the space between the two men grew shorter. The distance would be right for shooting now at any one of Grigg's steps.

'Wait a minute.' Cash heard Duke's low voice again, pitched so softly that he was surprised Griggs could hear it. Griggs hesitated in his walk, puzzled and angry, his hand edging nearer his gun butt.

Duke continued. 'What will happen to you when you die, Griggs? You know you're about to die.'

The words got to Griggs. They penetrated a chink in his

emotional armour and his face lost a fraction of its calculated calm. He reached for his gun.

Griggs made a splendid draw. Cash admired the tremendous, controlled speed and the fact that there wasn't a hairline of wasted motion.

But Griggs was dead before his gun barrel cleared leather.

Duke's hand was nothing but a flicker, the faint suggestion of a shadow of movement preceding the instant roar of his gun. His heavy slug caught Griggs in the middle of his chest and went on out, taking part of his back with it. Griggs pulled the trigger of his gun convulsively as he flew backward, but the shot was wild.

After it was over, Moss Hewitt was the first man in the street. He ran toward the corpse shouting, 'Murder! Murder! You saw it, Sheriff!'

'Looked like a fair fight to me.'

'I want you to arrest this man!' Hewitt pointed at Duke. 'It was a deliberate killing!'

Cash stepped down from the walk and met Hewitt as the trembling little man came up to Duke. 'That's enough talk about murder,' Cash said. 'You didn't hire Griggs to sweep floors in the Alhambra.'

Hewitt hissed, 'Are you going to do your duty?'

'The way I see it.'

Duke said, 'Maybe, Hewitt, you'd like to try to finish Grigg's hand?'

Hewitt's fury suddenly turned inside out and became fear. 'It was his fight, not mine.'

'Then shut up and get this obstacle out of the street,' Cash told him. 'It's interfering with traffic.'

Hewitt went to the corpse again as people streamed out onto the street to view the remains. Saul came running to Cash and Duke. 'I could see your lips movin', Duke,' he panted happily. 'Why all the chatter with Griggs before you shot him? You knew you had him cold.'

Duke put his gun back into its holster almost caressingly. 'You never know how fast the other fellow is, Saul. If you say the right thing to him at the right time you'll either scare him or make him mad. Either way you're stacking the

50

deck in your favour.' As much as it was possible for him to be, Duke was content. He turned to Cash and said, 'You still think you're good with a gun?'

Cash knew Duke was faster. He realized now what Saul had meant when he said gunplay was Duke's life. 'I'll say this, Duke. You may kick around this earth a long time, but when you die you'll have never lived except maybe eight or ten minutes. You really come alive, far as I can see, only during a shooting match.'

'That doesn't answer the question.'

'Maybe this will. I'm a damned good man with a gun. Griggs was so slow I felt downright sorry for him. I personally would have shot him through the head instead of ruining a perfectly good vest.'

Whitey Hall and Ben broke through the crowd around Griggs's body and came to where Cash, Duke, and Saul were standing apart from the others. Several people in the milling group followed him to hear what Whitey had to say.

'I just got the news, Sheriff,' he said with loud, sincere indignation. 'They tell me Duke shot a man. Is that right?'

Cash nodded seriously. 'He's lying right over there. Definitely shot.'

Whitey scowled and continued. 'Do you want to lock Duke up? Do you want me to post bond for him?'

'That won't be necessary, Mr. Hall. It was a plain case of self-defense.'

Two or three men in the group surrounding them voiced agreement. Whitey, mollified, said, 'Thank you, Sheriff. I'm glad to see you're right here on the job.' He walked away and Duke, giving Cash a hard look, followed him.

Cash walked up the street to cut over to the jail.

Williams was just coming out of the jailhouse. 'A man was killed,' he said as Cash walked up. 'You know about it?'

'Yes.'

'A pity. I'm sorry it happened.'

'Why? You know the man?'

'No. I don't need to know him to be sorry for him.'

'Believe me, the town is taking no loss. No matter which of the fighters had been killed, we all stood to be better off.'

'Did he have a family, a wife – anything?'

51

'How should I know?'

Williams drew a deep breath and sighed. 'I'm sorry if my questions are out of place. I don't know exactly what your job includes. I just thought maybe you made inquiries to find out who should be notified, things like that.'

'No. His name's Matt Griggs. Far as I know they're planting him right now. And no one cares.'

Williams looked at Cash carefully. He said, 'I do.'

'A man like Griggs doesn't want anybody to care about him.'

Williams was disturbed. 'You seem to know a lot about this man, after all. Why doesn't a man like Griggs want something to hold onto – something worth while? Is a man like that scared he won't measure up to anything decent? Is a gunfighter like Griggs really a coward?'

'You're talking like a preacher now.'

'I guess so. I get upset sometimes. It's too bad Griggs got killed before he got around to making any changes for the better.'

'He was trying to make a change for the better at the last minute. He was trying to kill another man just like him.'

'Well, maybe that's something.' Williams walked on the street and Cash went into the jailhouse.

In his desk there was an envelope containing five hundred-dollar bills. The bonus Hall had promised him. Whitey paid off quickly, and with no fuss.

CHAPTER FIVE

Cash took to staying up late nights and usually hauling three or four reluctant troublemakers off to jail. The average roaring drunk or tight-faced young punk looking for a fight caved right in at the sight of his badge. The Yellowrock *Weekly Times* ran a story on him, saying that he was doing a fine job and that everybody in town extended a warm welcome to him. A small note at the bottom of the page mentioned that Moss Hewitt had sold out the Alhambra and had left Yellowrock, and would be missed by hosts of friends.

Cash received invitations to talk at a couple of lady's clubs and a few of the town's leading families asked him to supper. He declined all such overtures, relieved that he had the understandable excuse of being too busy. At the end of his first three weeks, Cash figured he was making well over four hundred a month on arrests alone. Adding that to his official and unofficial salary and Whitey's occasional bonuses he could count on clearing around a thousand a month. He scribbled out the figures he'd written across the paper on the desk before him and tossed the pencil stub down. Not bad for an ex-brush popper who used to allow that times were good if he made a hundred dollars in five months.

Cash left his office and strolled out into the sunshine. On Fremont Street he saw Clem Clymer hurrying along, his eyes on the ground. 'Morning,' Cash said.

Clymer looked up and grinned. 'Howdy. Horrible hot day.'

'Too warm to be rushing the way you are.'

Clymer shook his head. 'Lots of things to do. Virginia's not working today and my place is buzzing.'

'Thought she worked on Fridays.'

'She does. But she's home with her youngster. The boy's sick.'

'What's the matter with him?'

'Don't know. You know how kids are. Running a fever.

53

Probably nothing, but she can't leave him. Well, I gotta trot.' The old man hurried on and Cash continued his leisurely walk. Too bad about that kid. Nice, the way the boy had given him the badge. It was probably important as hell to a young fellow like that. Cash remembered a time when he'd been sick as a boy. An uncle had brought him a set of toy soldiers. A silly little set of toy soldiers, yet Cash still couldn't look back at it without feeling in his chest a touch of the pleasure he'd felt those many years ago. About the time Cash got to thinking of Hank's mother, he happened to be in front of Bender's hardware store. He went in on the spur of the moment.

A tall, bald-headed man said, 'Top of the morning to you, Sheriff. Can I help you?'

'What have you got in, oh, say about a forty-four single-shot rifle?'

'Couple of nice models here. Got a single-shot Henry, and Spencer puts out a nice gun, a little lighter stock and brass-tipped hunting sights. I also got a Collier's over-and-under forty-four that's a few years older and I can let you have it at a good price.'

'Let's see a new Spencer.' Cash tested the gun's weight and the feel of its grip in his hands. 'What'll you take for this?'

'That'll run nineteen dollars.'

'Give me a couple of cartons of shells to go with it.'

Fifteen minutes later Cash picked up his buckskin on Corral Street and rode out of town. After an hour and a half he crested the top of the hill above the Brendan place. No one was in sight. He walked the buck down the slope and started to tie him at the hitching-post. Hank's mother stepped onto the porch as he finished hitching the reins. She had a weary slant to her shoulders and her eyes were tired.

He said, 'They tell me your boy is feeling under the weather.'

She sat on the porch step and said, 'That man Sullivan had a mare that ran away when he was shot. Hank was looking for her. Four days ago he found her. She'd got her loop reins tangled in some brush and was nearly dead. He managed to get her back here and we tried to doctor her

54

back to health, but it was just about impossible. Hank exhausted himself working on her. Night before last she got out of the stable and wandered up into the hills. We found her there, dead. Then yesterday he started to run a fever. Today it's worse.'

'It'll probably pass, Mrs. Brendan. Kids run a fever easy.'

She stood and smiled, tossing her head so the red hair fell smoothly across her shoulders. 'Come on in.'

Hank lay on the bottom bunk, a gray homespun blanket over him. He was looking toward the door, and when Cash entered the room he whispered, 'I ain't really sick.'

'You're doing a good job of play-acting then.' His mother straightened the blanket and put her hand softly on his forehead. After a moment she straightened back up. 'Excuse me, I'll be back in a minute.'

When she'd gone out the door, Cash straddled a chair near Hank's bunk and said, 'You had some trouble with a horse?'

'Yeah. That's what I meant when I said I ain't sick. I just don't feel so good. I feel bad about that poor horse. And I feel worse about the fellow that owned her.'

'You got to face up to things. Sometimes it's hard, but you've got to do what'll pay off best. Running yourself down till you're in bed won't do you any good.'

His mother came in carrying a bucket of water. With both hands she started to lift it onto the table. Cash, who had stood when she came in, reached out a hand and lifted it for her.

'Thanks, Mr. Jefferson,' she said.

'I hardly know who you're talking to when you use that name. I prefer Cash.'

'All right. Please call me Virginia.'

Cash went out to the buckskin and took the Spencer from the saddle. Back in the house he showed the rifle to Hank. 'I was thinking I'd get your opinion on this gun – if you feel up to looking it over.'

The boy shifted to a sitting position and said, 'Boy, you sure own nice things. That looks brand new.'

'It's not too old. Fellow who gave it to me says it's a late model.'

Hank worked with the bolt action for a moment and,

finally lifting it to the right position, pulled it back. 'It's fine,' he said.

'Trouble with it is, it's only a single-shot.' Cash straddled the chair again and said thoughtfully, 'I've got my Winchester lever action, so I don't need another rifle. Especially a single-shot. But a one-shot gun is the best for learning on. Fellow picks up the knack of shooting straight if he hasn't but one shell to count on.' He studied the back of his hand briefly, then looked back at Hank. 'I was thinking maybe you'd like to take that gun off my hands.'

Hank's face glowed. 'I sure would.' He shot the bolt back and examined the weapon with sparkling eyes. 'I sure would!'

'It's yours.'

Virginia put a steaming cup of coffee on the table beside Cash. 'Dinner will be ready soon. Then, Hank, you try to sleep for an hour. Then if you feel a little better, maybe Cash will take you out a little while and show you how to use the rifle. If he has time.'

'I've got time.'

When Hank was down for a nap, Cash and Virginia walked to a grove of trees near the house. They sat on a fallen log and Virginia said, 'I think his fever's broken. His face was cooler. It was good of you to bring him that gun.' She leaned back against a birch tree and brought one leg up to fold her arms around it. 'Is your job going well?'

'Fair.'

'Everyone I've talked to seems to think you're a good man. They say the town's quieter than it's ever been.'

'I like the job.'

Virginia stood and thrust her hands into her pockets. She looked at the buckskin Cash had unsaddled and roped to a tree where he could feed himself on sweet-grass. 'That's a good-looking horse. Must stand seventeen hands high.'

'Sixteen-two.'

'What's his name?'

'Never got around to giving him one.'

'Why, it's criminal not to name a fine animal like that. You should be ashamed.' She smiled. 'We'll name him right now. My two horses up in the stable are called Thunder and Lightning, so you can't have those two names.

But that still leaves several others.' She looked thoughtful. 'I've got a good one. How about Gold?'

'Gold? He does look like a nugget that hasn't been washed off.'

'It will make you both sound like the wealthiest man and horse in the territory. Cash and Gold. It almost sounds as though you could be put in a bank at a good interest rate.'

'All right. Gold it is. And I'll deposit us at the Yellowrock bank tomorrow.'

Hank came to the door and called, 'I can't sleep any more. And I feel better.'

Cash showed the boy how to load and fire and throw out the spent shell. Then he explained how to line up the sights. Hank tried a shot at a rock sitting up on the hill and overshot by six feet. 'There's a little kick to it,' he said, rubbing his shoulder.

On his fourth try Hank hit the rock and yelled with joy as the bullet whined off it. Cash grinned and patted his shoulder. 'You've got a good eye and a good hand. You'll teach yourself the rest.'

'What about side guns like the two you're wearing?' Hank asked. 'They harder to use?'

'In a way. But the basic truth holds true with all guns. Good shooting means speed and accuracy, and if you've got to sacrifice one, be sure it isn't accuracy. I've seen a man draw and shoot four times before the other pulled his first shot. The first man was a heck of a lot quicker, and everybody agreed he was pretty fast the next day when they were burying him. You get your accuracy. Then build as much speed as you can on top of it.'

They started back to the cabin and Hank said, 'Up at Bancroft one of the stage drivers said you'd most likely be workin' for a man named Whitey Hall. It didn't sound too good, the way he said it. I've been thinkin' about it, and I'm glad you got to be sheriff instead.'

'Why?'

'Well, it's a big thing, being sheriff, don't you think?'

'It's okay, I guess.'

'Cash,' Virginia called, hearing their steps on the porch. 'Can you stay for supper?'

'I ought to be getting back to town.'

57

'Please do stay. And Hank, you crawl back into that bunk. I don't want you to push yourself too much.'

Supper was done and Hank put to sleep by eight o'clock. Virginia walked out with Cash and held a lantern while he saddled up. Finished, he slapped the horse's shoulder and said, 'You're not just a buckskin stallion any more boy. You're a special animal with a name.'

'Gold,' Virginia said. 'I like that.'

Far away in the hills a coyote called piteously to the moon – a long, sad wailing that tapered off into nothing.

She shuddered. 'I hate it when they howl that way.'

'Why?'

'It's spooky. I always think of what they told me when I was a little girl back East. Howling like that means someone is going to die.'

'That's been proven true out here in the West. Man I knew used to say that the coyotes knew if death was coming. And sure enough, after they'd been wailing steady around his cabin for forty years, one night he up and died.'

Virginia smiled and said, 'You're making fun of me.'

'Not really.'

'I don't quite understand you.' Her voice was suddenly low and puzzled. 'I can't be sure. But you seem almost afraid of me.'

'I guess I am, in a way. I've never had anything to do with a woman like you. Before, when I was doing – other things – I wouldn't have tried to pass a word with you. I'm glad I feel able to now. But I don't know why I feel able to, and I'm still probably a little scared.' He mounted Gold and called, 'Adios,' as he rode out of the circle of lamplight.

Cash rode into Yellowrock at shortly after ten. He'd started to make a round of the town on foot when Saul walked up fast behind him and said, 'You better see Whitey at the Alamo. Take the lead outa your boots.'

In the familiar back office he poured himself a drink while Whitey stared past him at the doorway, drumming his fingernails sharply on the desk.

As Cash lowered his empty glass, Whitey said, 'I've been trying to get you for an hour.'

'I've been unavailable all day.'

'I want you available'

Cash grinned. 'Careful. Remember you're talking to the sheriff.'

'Don't forget who made you sheriff. And who can break you like that!' Whitey snapped his fingers. 'Deputy marshal was in town looking for you today. As head of the city council I saw him in your absence. He left a bunch of official papers and forms in your office. And he says you're under the jurisdiction of the circuit court up in Grandville. Judge sits there the last day of every month. Any law-breakers you want to go before a judge, you'll take up there.'

'A little thing like his visit didn't whip you up this much.'

'That's right. At the faro table out front there's a two-bit wrangler whose good luck is running too long. He's into the house for about fifteen thousand.'

'Now that's a little more upsetting. How come your boys let him buck the house that far? I know they can't deal a cold deck in faro, but I'm surprised they didn't boot him out long ago.'

'It was an accident. The dealer thought his luck would break and it didn't. Everybody's paying attention to him now, so I can't have the boys rough him up. It'd be bad for my reputation. But sure as hell nobody's going to walk out of here with fifteen thousand of my dollars. And he laughed in my face when I went out and told him he ought to quit.'

'That was unfriendly of him.'

'No one laughs at me. I want you to get out of here and come back in the front way. Make it look like a legal visit but pick a fight with him. I don't want him just thrown into jail. I want him hurt. Hurt him all you want. Claim you got the word that he was working partners with my dealer.'

'Will your dealer go along with that?'

'You're damned right he will. Unless he's tired of living.'

Cash circled around the ally and back onto Front Street. Coming into the Alamo, he saw that most of the customers were grouped around the corner table. As he stepped toward the table the group roared with laughter and began to break-up. A big, half-drunk cowboy wearing worn levis,

59

and a battered old army hat stood up from the faro table, leaned his head back and yelled, 'I'm a wirehaired wolf down from the Dragoons – and I say any poor son with dust on his tongue can step right up to the water trough here and wash it down on me!'

After two more steps toward the bar the puncher raised his head back once more, and filled with the sheer joy of living, let loose with a head-splitting cowboy yell. 'Yahhh-hoo! I'm a wild mustang that's never been broke! I'm a maverick longhorn lookin' for a fight!'

'That won't be hard to find.' Cash's voice slapped clearly across the room.

The puncher looked at Cash, and at his star. He smiled good-naturedly. 'I ain't lookin' for a scrap, Sheriff. That's just glad talk. I won myself more money tonight than I ever knew there was in this world. Come on and have a drink with me and my friends. It's my pleasure. My name's Brady.'

'Neither of us will be having a drink, Brady.'

The cowboy's face tilted to one side in bewilderment. He glanced around him at the people he'd invited to the bar, then back to Cash. 'Anythin' wrong, Sheriff?'

'I'd say so. You and the dealer were playing partners against the house.'

Brady didn't lose his temper or get excited. He simply tried to explain. He said, 'But that ain't true, Sheriff. I ain't never been in this town before tonight and don't even know that dealer's name. Someone lied to you.'

'You got it all wrong, Sheriff,' a man in the crowd said. 'This fellow ain't good enough to be a pro. He –'

'Be quiet!' Cash commanded. 'I'm calling him a cheat!'

Brady took a deep breath. He now seemed to understand, and he looked tired. 'Seems you're pushin' at me awful hard, mister. I ain't much with a gun. But you'll have to take mine away 'fore I'll be bait for your local hoosegow.'

The group surrounding Brady moved out of the line of fire, and he grinned sadly. 'It just don't seem to do a body no good to lay his hands on some money. I'm waitin', Sheriff.'

Cash remembered what Whitey had said about hurting

60

the puncher. Now, facing him, he felt as bad as Brady looked. How could you hurt a man who was waiting to draw with his hand held at an awkward angle a foot and a half from his gun? 'Why don't you come peacefully, Brady?'

'You pushed me. This is your hand, Sheriff. I ain't gonna back down.'

'Look, Brady – ' Cash unconsciously twisted his wrist slightly forward as he started to try to reason with the man. Inexperienced and nervous, Brady misread the tiny gesture and went for his gun. His heavy hand slammed to the butt of his revolver and actually pushed the gun down into the holster before starting its upward motion. Cash's gun leaped lightly into his hand and roared once.

Brady's gun was so far from clearing leather that it plopped back into its holster as his fingers left their grip on it. He cried sharply in pain and grabbed his right shoulder with his left hand.

Cash put his Colt back and walked to Brady. 'Can you get to the jail on your own feet?'

Brady's teeth were clenched so tightly with pain that he couldn't speak. It looked to Cash as if there were rims of tears in the man's eyes. He blinked and nodded.

Whitey came into the centre of the crowd. 'I'll take the responsibility for my employee, Sheriff.'

Brady looked from Whitey to Cash. Releasing his grip on his injured shoulder momentarily, he fumbled in his shirt and brought out the thick roll of folding money he'd won. He threw it on the floor in front of Whitey, then followed Cash slowly out to Front Street.

At the jail, Cash lit the lamp and told Brady to lie down in an open cell in the back. As the sputtering flame took hold, Cash saw a river of blood left across the front office by the cowboy. He'd had no idea the arm was bleeding so. He started out the door and met the hook-nosed man, Winterburg, coming in.

'Brought Joe Gaines with me,' Winterburg said. 'Owns the Longbranch and tends bar there. Knows medicine.'

Gaines was stocky, quiet and efficient looking. He carried a worn leather bag with him. 'Fetch that light on back,' he said.

Cash set the lamp up in the cell where Brady was lying. The cowboy was sweating now and had his teeth clenched. Whenever they loosened their hold on each other his high, tortured breathing became a low cry of agony.

Gaines ripped the shirt away from the shoulder and said, 'Bring that light right here.' Winterburg reached for it and held it beside Brady. Gaines opened the bag beside him and took a long, thin instrument from it.

'Anything I can do?' said Cash.

'Reckon not,' Gaines muttered.

Cash walked into the shadows of the front office and sat on his desk. After a while he heard Gaines say in a low voice, 'This is going to hurt like hell, fella.'

Brady screamed then, a short scream that pierced the air keenly and echoed dimly in the still air of the jail-house.

Twenty minutes later, Gaines and Winterburg came into the front office. 'You got any whisky?' Gaines asked.

'Not here. I'll get some.'

'I'll get it.' Winterburg disappeared through the door.

Cash settled back on the desk. 'How is he?'

'I've seen 'em better off.'

Cash mumbled, 'I had time. So I just clipped him in the shoulder.'

'Maybe you did him a favour. Maybe not.'

'What do you mean, maybe?'

'You ever see a shoulder bone hit with a lead slug?'

'No.'

'I should have had you take a look. The whole socket's smashed. Pieces of the slug and the bone all through the shoulder. Got most of it out. No need to cut his arm off, but he'll never use it again. He'll go through life with it hanging useless.'

'You sure?' Cash's lips were dry. 'Doctors work wonders these days.'

'None of them are making bone joints.'

Winterburg came back with the bottle. 'Okay if I leave the whole thing with him, Joe?'

'Yeah,' Gaines nodded. 'Help him take a long shot or two right now. Tell him he can have the rest when he wakes up.'

In a few minutes Winterburg came out carrying the lamp. 'He's asleep.' He put the lamp on the desk and faced Cash. 'If it makes you feel good, I've got to admit you're damned handy with a gun.'

Gaines breathed a long, low sigh and said, 'Don't ride him. We're on edge because it was pretty messy. I just got through blowin' off myself. But damn it, Jefferson was doing just exactly what we hired him for.' He clapped Cash wearily on the shoulder. 'I'm sorry for what I said.'

'I'm not sorry.' Winterburg said. 'I was there. I saw it happen. You called him a cheat. You pushed him into a fight. From where I stood it looked like you was out for a little target practice.'

'I'm sorry if it looked that way.'

'It did.' Winterburg stalked out the door. Gaines picked up his bag and said, 'Winterburg's feelin' bad. He'll calm down. Don't worry about it, Sheriff. You've got to do your job as you see it.'

Cash put out the lamp and sat alone in the darkness most of the night. Toward morning Brady's breathing became regular and slow. Then Cash got up and went to his room at the Holiday.

He unbuckled his guns slowly and slung them over the footboard of his bed. Roughly, he began to pull off his shirt. Under the pressure, the pin of the badge popped loose and scratched his arm as Cash jerked the shirt off. Cash swore and threw the shirt on the floor.

He was awakened a few hours later by a knock. He opened the door and the room clerk said timidly, 'Mr. Hall to see you, Mr. Jefferson. He's downstairs in the lobby.'

There were several other people in the lobby. Hall got up from his chair as Cash entered and said loudly, 'Sheriff, I'm not here as chairman of the city council, this morning, but as a plain businessman who wants to thank you for doing a fine job last night.'

Cash said tightly, 'All in a day's work.'

They went out to the street. Walking toward the jail, Whitey said in a lower voice, 'Saw Joe Gaines this morning. He tells me that smart punk will be crippled for the rest of his life.'

63

'Yes.'

'Good work. You did the job right. I don't want you to get the idea that every time you make a move you get paid extra for it, but I can't let a job like that go unrewarded. You can figure on another couple hundred.'

'What about your faro dealer?'

'Naturally he admitted the whole thing. Since he was so willing to cooperate I'm not going to press charges against him. But I want to see Brady charged with intent to defraud and resisting an officer. Maybe we can stretch that to attempted murder. He went for his gun. You can take him up to the circuit court at the end of the month.'

'When someone riles you, you stay riled, don't you?'

'Nobody laughs at me or throws money on the floor in front of me. He'll be one sorry saddletramp before I'm finished with him.'

At Corral Street, Whitey stopped. 'I'll leave you here.'

'So long.' Cash continued to the jail.

Brady was awake and sitting up. The whisky bottle beside him was two-thirds empty. When he saw Cash he stared at him long and hard. Then he grinned a slight, lopsided grin and said. 'Drink, Sheriff?'

'After what I did last night?'

Brady glanced briefly at the thick bandages binding his right shoulder and holding the top of his arm firmly against his torso. 'Never saw so much fuss over a man's gettin' nicked. Though I must say it hurt some.'

'Last night was a bad night for you, Brady.'

'I reckon. Started out lookin' pretty good. But as I recollect I didn't hang onto that big, beautiful roll very long.'

Cash said, 'That shoulder of yours is bad hit. They tell me you won't have the use of your arm.'

Brady thought about that for a while. He slowly put his good hand up and rubbed it back across his hair. 'They sure?'

'Yes.'

'A passel of ramrods can swear to the fact that I ain't never been much of a cowboy with two arms. Reckon this puts me right smack at the bottom of the barrel.'

'Your horse need looking after?'

'No. I didn't just hitch 'im. I left him in a stable.' Brady picked up the bottle and handed it to Cash. 'Drink?'

'Thanks.' Cash tipped the bottle and handed it back.

'Also, as I recollect,' Brady said, 'I'm in this here calaboose of yours for trying to bust the house last night with the help of that skinny-faced dealer.'

'Yes.'

'Somebody was talkin' with a mighty crooked tongue. Truth is I never thought of such a thing, though it ain't a bad idea.'

'The dealer admitted the whole thing. Said you were both in on it.'

'I'm tellin' you straight that it ain't so, but I don't guess my word will cut much ice.'

'You'll get a fair hearing up to Grandville at the end of the month.'

Brady took a drink from the bottle and lay slowly back on his bunk, his eyes closed tightly and his face toward the wall. He muttered, 'I guess that's the best a fellow can ask for – a fair hearin'. Thanks, Sheriff.'

CHAPTER SIX

Cash arranged with a restaurant to take Brady's meals to him. Then he went to the bar at the Oriental and started to drink. He spent most of the next few days supporting the Oriental and getting used to the fact that being drunk wasn't as pleasureable as it used to be.

One night, heading back for the jail, he was approached by Williams. The preacher said, 'Jefferson, you're as high as a kite.'

'The view's lovely when you're this high.'

Williams fell in with him. 'What I want to know is, when a town only has one sheriff, who runs him in when he gets drunk?'

'He takes himself to jail, which is what I'm doing right now.'

'It's too bad about that man Brady being injured permanently. But you can't blame yourself for that.'

'I can't seem to do anything to please you, Preacher. A while back I didn't give a damn about a shooting and you took exception. Now you're down on me because you think a shooting's got under my hide.'

'It wasn't your fault you hit him where you did. That bullet was in the hand of God.'

'No.' Cash shook his head loosely. 'It was in the shoulder of Brady.'

'And now it's in the head of Cash. That one slug seems to have hit all over the place.'

'My shooting's phenomenal. But you're wrong. I don't give a hang about Brady.'

'Go a cup of strong coffee?'

Cash paused, then shrugged and said, 'Why not? Your company can't be worse than the barman's at the Oriental. All he ever says is, "You're drinking as if you just got in off the Great Desert." If I hadn't been the sheriff, the pride and joy of Yellowrock, I'd have shot him the last time he said that.'

'Come on.' Williams pointed Cash up Allen Street and they went into the church and to his quarters in the back.

Cash glanced about at the finished walls and new ceiling. 'You don't have to worry about the rain any more.'

'No. Pretty soon I'll be able to relax long enough to start worrying about my real business.'

Williams put a mug of coffee in front of Cash and poured one for himself. 'I've known you going on six weeks now. I'd say you've changed since we rode in on that stage together.'

'I was drunk then. I'm drunk now. I guess I'm even a little drunker, if that's what you mean by change.'

Williams grinned. 'I'd guess you're getting drunk for different reasons these days.'

'No one can say why another man takes to liquor. I just happen to get thirsty awful easy.'

'Maybe. But I'd still say you're sorry the man in your jail is crippled. And furthermore, I'd say it wouldn't have bothered you much a while back.'

'You're not trying to tell me I'm getting religion?'

Williams studied the coffee in his cup. 'No. Not religion. But you're getting something, I'll tell you that. You're a bigger man now than when you got into town.'

Cash grunted. 'All the sitting around I've been doing, I probably put on a layer of fat.' He pushed his hat back on his head, irritated and uncomfortable when Williams ignored his joking manner. 'What the hell makes you say a loco thing like that? You hardly know me.'

'A couple of things. Like a piano player you saved from having his head knocked in. Like the rifle you gave a kid named Hank Brendan.'

'How'd you know about those things?'

'The piano player offered to play the organ in church when we get one – before he left town, that is. And I was out to see the families in Spangle Valley. Saw Mrs. Brendan and the boy. They speak highly of you. They wouldn't have spoken highly of the man who came in on the stage-coach.'

'And what in hell could have caused this wondrous switch in me, which is only in your head, to come about?'

Williams pursed his lips. 'You got me.' He looked up at Cash thoughtfully. 'Maybe a lot of things. My guess would be wearing that badge.'

Cash stood up angrily and walked to the door. Opening it, he turned back and said, 'All this talk about people changing is fool talk. It'll be a freezing day in Hades before you find me doing an about-face.'

Williams came to the door and leaned against the frame. 'I can have my own opinions.'

'Not when they're as wrong as yours are. You make a living being handy with souls. I make a living being handy with guns. And no preacher can understand a gunman, whichever side of the badge he happens to be on. It just isn't possible. They have nothing in common.'

'Every man has things in common with every other man.'

'No.' Cash shook his head. 'I'd like to see me give a talk from a pulpit. Or I'd like to see you look good with a gun.'

'Those are nice guns you wear. May I see one?'

Cash hesitated, then handed the Colt in his left holster to Williams. The little man took it cautiously, in both hands. 'Haven't held one for quite a while,' he explained. At the side of the churchyard where the ground sloped up to the mountains, a fence of thin white pickets had been put up. Williams shifted the revolver gingerly to his right hand and the gun suddenly looked at home. He stared at the pickets, cold gray in the bright moonlight.

The revolver roared and the top of a picket on the gate in the middle of the fence disappeared. The gun boomed four more times and the four remaining pickets on the gate were stunted in a good straight line.

Williams handed the gun back to Cash. 'I've been meaning to cut that gate down about a foot anyway. Good night.' He went in and shut the door behind him.

Cash stared at the pickets. He whistled soundlessly and holstered his gun. Then he walked back to the jail.

Friday night the waiter from the Tip Top had brought in Brady's supper and had just left when Ma Bracken, despite her bulk, lumbered swiftly into the front office. 'Sheriff, you got time to help me?' she panted. 'Bunch of miners are bustin' up my place!'

'Let's go stop them.' Cash strode out with the heavy woman hurrying along beside him.

'Way it is,' she said, gasping for breath, 'the powder

monkeys and pick-benders got a feud on. Yesterday a charge of dynamite dropped some rocks on some diggers and a couple of them got hurt. Some say there was too much explosive used. Some say the diggers was too close. Anyway, there's a bunch of 'em in my place about to settle it when I come for you.'

They could hear the fight going on a block away. When they were a hundred feet from the little cafe, Cash told Ma Bracken to wait and started for the door. A table crashed out the front window as he passed it and he ducked down as shattered glass fell around him.

He charged through the doorway into a riotous jungle of flying fists, boots and chairs. His shouted command to stop was not even heard. A moment later a hard blow caught him on the side of the head and knocked him down. He pitched back onto his feet and plowed into the centre of the fight, his fists walloping a pathway before him.

In the middle of the room he sidestepped a bushy-faced, onrushing miner and sank his right into the man's stomach. Dodging a chair that flashed down at him, he kicked the legs of the man who held it out from under him. He was in the centre of a tiny clearing now, and he drew both guns and fired them into the air. The roaring blasts thundered through the room and the hesitant fighters turned toward him slightly, caught in numerous fighting stances.

'Next man makes a move, it'll be his last,' Cash said quietly. 'Now line up against the wall there. All of you.'

One burly young man grumbled, 'Them damned diggers started it.'

'We was eatin', mindin' our own business, when that gang of powder monkeys come in lookin' for trouble,' another retorted.

'Line up,' Cash repeated.

There were about twenty men altogether. They stood against the wall glaring sulkily at Cash as Ma Bracken came in and started to wail over the wreckage the battle had left. 'You bums!' she exploded. 'This will ruin me! You had no right to come to an old woman's place and smash it up like this! No right at all.' Her big, homely face burst into tears and she put her hands up to hide her grief.

'How much you figure it'll cost to put your place back

in shape?' Cash put his guns back in their holsters.

She wiped her eyes and said, 'The front window's about forty dollars. All to itself.'

'That's a start.'

Ma Bracken figured the damage at about two hundred dollars.

'Now have you boys any notion how to square accounts?' Cash asked.

Some of the men in the long line shuffled their feet apologetically, and one of them said, 'I'm sorry, Ma. It's a damn shame your place got busted up.' Another said defiantly, 'One of them diggers hit me first. I had to defend myself.'

Cash counted noses. Altogether there were twenty-three men against the wall. 'I figure that if each one of you kicks in ten bucks it'll come out about right. You just file past here and drop off the money one at a time. If you haven't got a ten spot Ma will take your name. And if you haven't paid up the kitty by next payday I'll come to collect personally.'

When the line had worked its way to the end, Ma Bracken had a hundred and eighty dollars and five names. Cash picked up a chair and set it right. 'You let me know if those five men don't pay up.' He started to go out.

'Sheriff,' she called in a small voice surprisingly unlike her normal throaty grumble.

'Yes?'

'You just sit down here a minute.' She brought the chair he'd set right and put it near him. 'Your eye will be black as tar come mornin' if it ain't seen to.'

Cash sat down and she brought a cold, folded rag. 'Hold that to it while I wet a fresh one.'

After the third cold pack, Cash said, 'That ought to hold the swelling down. Much obliged.'

'Since this ain't much of a place,' she said, 'most lawmen I've knowed would've just let that fight peter out. A few might've stopped it and tossed everybody out on the street. You're the only one I know would've done what you did. I thank you.'

'Forget it.'

'Another thing. Talk around town has it you plugged that

fellow in the Alamo 'cause you like shootin'. But after the way you handled yourself tonight, I know it ain't so. You could have just as leave busted wide loose with them hog-legs after you warned the boys to stop. But I seen you was careful not to hit anythin' but the ceilin'.'

'Thanks for tending to my eye.' Cash stepped out to the street, where a curious crowd had gathered around the ring of broken glass that had been the front window. As he moved through the crowd, someone in the circle of men called out, 'Hey, Sheriff! You step into a door?'

Another man, closer to him, shouted, 'Hell, boy, you should've seen the other twenty fellows!'

The crowd broke into laughter and Cash shoved on through, grinning in spite of himself.

Back at the jail, Brady called to him from his cell. He went to the back of the building and said, 'What is it?'

'I don't care a lot any more, tell you the truth, but who put you onto me that night? Who said I was in cahoots with the dealer?'

'I can't give out that kind of information, Brady. Besides, the dealer turned evidence. That's all that's needed.'

'Five'll get you ten the one who told you is a sidekick to that white-haired wolf who owns the joint.'

'What makes you think so?'

'I mean he didn't want to lose a pot of money, that's all. But he had to have some flunky give you the word. Then he tells the dealer he'd damned well better say he was playin' partners with me. That way he'd get his money back and he's in the clear.'

'That's a long shot, Brady.'

'Well – ' Brady sagged down on his cot. 'Like I say, I don't really care much any more. Just figured I'd mention it.'

'If you get out of this right side up – if the judge sitting circuit court finds you not guilty, say, what will you do, Brady?'

'Oh, I reckon I'd go back home to Nebraska. A kid brother and my old man got a place out there. It'd be kinda good to see them.' Brady stared off into space, then came out of his short reverie. 'But I got a slim chance of that, and you know it, Sheriff.'

Two days before the end of the month, Whitey Hall brought the dealer to Cash's office. 'His name's Prentis, and he'll give you all the testimony you need. Got his statement here. I figure with a good word from you he'll get either an acquittal or a suspended sentence. That drifter in the back cell there won't get off so easy.' Whitey handed Cash a copy of a letter. 'The council secretary wrote to Grandville last week to tell them you'd be there with these two.'

Prentis was a sharp-faced, jittery little man. 'It's all in them papers,' he said nervously. 'How he talked me into doing it. He even threatened me. I never been in trouble before. Mr. Hall has got some important people to write statements that my character's always been good. Above reproach. It's all in them papers.'

'Guess you've got nothing to be nervous about, then.' Cash said.

'Nope. Nothing to be nervous about. Nothing at all. It's all in the papers.'

Prentis's horse was brought to the front of the jail as Whitey walked out. Cash picked up Gold, then went to the stable on Fremont where Brady's horse was being kept.

They rode out of town at eleven o'clock, Brady and Prentis side by side and Cash slightly behind them.

Shortly before sundown Cash picked a spot near a spring to make camp. Working with only one arm, Brady took longer to unpack his saddle roll, and the other two walked a few steps to the spring for a drink of water.

'Better keep your eye on Brady,' Cash warned Prentis. 'He's got a mean look about him.'

A few minutes later Prentis was leaning down to start the fire. He turned to judge the distance that separated him from Brady. He was safe. He turned back to the fire.

A clap of thunder engulfed him as something solid crashed against his head. He fell limply forward, his thin chest crushing the twigs he'd gathered together.

Behind him Cash put his gun back and turned to Brady. 'That was a cowardly blow,' he said, 'hitting a man when his back's turned that way.'

Brady straightened up from where he'd been laying out

72

his bedroll. Puzzled, he said, 'What'd you clobber that little punk for, Sheriff?'

'I didn't. You did. And just before that you slugged me in exactly the same way. We're both as unconscious as hell.'

'What are you gettin' at?'

'I mean you're free to do anything you want. And if I had to decide in your place, I'd get on my horse and clear out of here before either of us wakes up.'

Brady walked slowly up to Cash. 'You know the truth? That I'm bein' stampeded into a jail sentence?'

'Yes.'

Brady shook his head. 'I ain't gonna run. I appreciate what you're doin' for me, but I ain't gonna run. I'd be on the prod the rest of my life. I'd rather face up to it now and get it done with.' Brady's level eyes suddenly probed Cash with new interest. 'Did you know it was a railroadin' when you shot me?'

It was hard for Cash to answer. He looked at Brady's injured arm and said, 'Quit asking stupid questions. Get your stuff on your horse and high-tail it out of here.'

'You knew,' Brady said quietly. 'What I'm wonderin' now is whether you got any good reason to get this man out of the way and then shoot me in the back – as if I was tryin' to get away from you.'

'I could shoot you right now. I wouldn't have to wait for you to turn your back.'

Brady muttered, 'Maybe you mean it. But they'd have my name and description goin' all over the country on the telegraph.'

'I'm the one who'd send out a description. I'm busy and won't get to it for a long time. When I do I'll say your real name is John Smith and you're ninety years old, bald, short, and cross-eyed. Damn it! Get your stuff on your horse and get going!'

'You know, I feel real sorry for you, Sheriff.' Brady's voice was low and intense. 'You're the flunky I was talkin' about a while back without knowin' it. You poor, dirty coward. Now that you've wrecked my arm you're too yellow to see me go to jail on top of it.'

'You're talking too much, Brady.'

73

'You ain't got the insides to be a first-rate son of a bitch. How much was in it for you? It must have been kind of funny watchin' me grab around for that old gun of mine that ain't never been used for nothin' much but a hammer. It's really a big deal on your part now, offerin' to leave me go.'

'That's better than I'd do for most. Move along.'

Brady started to reroll his blankets. Cash began to help him, but the cowboy wouldn't take his help. When he was finally ready, Brady swung awkwardly into saddle and reined his horse around to face Cash. He sat his horse wordlessly, staring down at the sheriff. He looked as though he were about to say something, but he didn't. Finally he turned his mount east and spurred it ahead. At the top of a near hill his silhouette stood out against the skyline for a brief second, and then disappeared among the night shadows.

Cash turned Prentis over with his boot and slapped him twice. The little gambler sputtered, choked and then cried, 'What? What?'

'I asked you to help me watch Brady!' Cash snarled. 'You let him go after he clubbed me.'

'But he was fifteen feet from me,' Prentis moaned.

'Stop making excuses. Build that fire. No point chasing him in the middle of the night.'

When the flames were springing up through the twigs and small branches the little man said, 'Are we going to go on to Grandville all the same?'

'Certainly. You're booked for trial there, the same as Brady.'

'Will – will this make any difference? I mean in the trial?'

'You can never tell.'

Cash rode back into Yellowrock three days later. He was alone. Within half an hour Whitey Hall came into the jailhouse. He smiled and said, 'How did it go? What did Brady get?'

Cash said, 'Man by the name of Judge Harris sits circuit court at Grandville. He is about as mean as any man I ever saw.'

'Good. What did he give Brady?'

'Nothing. Brady slugged me from behind and that dumb dealer of yours let him get away. I suspect he's halfway to Mexico City by now.'

Whitey's eyes narrowed. 'Damned careless of you. Letting a one-armed man take you. Where's Prentis?'

'Like I say, that Harris is a tough nut. He allowed since one of the two got away he'd hit the other one twice as hard. Prentis is starting three years in jail at Yuma.'

'Damn it, dealers aren't easy to find,' Whitey fumed. 'I'd say this is the first time you've done a thoroughly bad job. I don't like it.'

'Sorry.'

Whitey stamped out of the jail and Cash put his feet on the desk. He was sitting there, studying the wall before him, when Clem Clymer came in. The old man sat down wordlessly and wiped the sweat from his forehead with a large, red bandana. 'Hot,' he finally volunteered.

'No hotter than usual.'

'It's usually pretty hot.'

Clymer lapsed back into silence. Then he cleared his throat and said, 'I just dropped by to invite you to a party. Sort of a before-the-weddin' thing. Bill Grayson is getting married. Finally got a girl to say yes to him.'

'Oh.' Cash's lungs seemed to be temporarily short on air. He breathed some in and said, 'Virginia Brendan?'

Clymer leaned back in his chair and pushed his lips into a thoughtful curve. 'As a matter of fact, no. He kind of gave up with her, it seems. Don't know why. But Harriet Borland, daughter to that fellow on the council who recommended you for sheriff, has said she'd tie the knot with him. So I'm gettin' a bunch of people together at my place next Friday to celebrate.'

'Maybe I'll be able to stop in for a while. Thanks for asking me.'

Clymer stood up. 'Good. Speaking of Virginia – as you were – it seems to me she's got no escort for Friday. I'm not sure, but it just seems to me. She's working at the store today in case you'd like to put in your bid.'

'I'll do that. I'll go along with you now.' He got up and walked out into the hot sun with Clymer.

At Clymer's Dry Goods Emporium, Virginia was

75

straightening bolts of cloth on the counter before her. She smiled as they came in, and the old man, tipping his hat, continued on into the back office.

'I've been wondering when I'd get a chance to try my sales talk on the sheriff,' she said. 'What can I sell you today?'

'I could use some shirts.'

'Shirts like those you wear will have to be ordered specially.'

'I've been thinking that mine are a little too colorful. I'm tired of fancy ones. I'd like something in just plain white or black, or gray, maybe.'

'That's more in our line. And we have some fine styles in good materials. Just in from California.' She laid some shirts out on the counter.

'What do you like?' Cash asked her.

She chose three white, two black and a gray. 'I like these. They're about your size, aren't they?'

'Yes. Now, if I wanted to take a girl to a party and impress her with my almost unbelievable charm, which of them would you suggest to go with a plain black dress coat?'

'That's easy. This white. With a black or red string tie you'd be all the rage.'

Cash nodded. 'That ought to please the girl, all right.'

'I assure you it would.' Virginia took a black string tie from the shelf behind her and laid it out at the throat of the shirt. 'Now just imagine your head lying on the counter next to the shirt,' she said. 'Doesn't that make a lovely picture?'

Cash grinned and put money for the purchase on the counter. 'I forgot to mention that I don't actually have a girl for the party. It's the one Mr. Clymer is having. I was wondering if you might go with me.'

Virginia put the black tie back on the shelf and replaced it with a red one. 'I personally prefer red,' she told him. 'You may pick me up at seven.'

Cash took his shirts to his hotel room and lay down for a short nap. He awakened at about six, had supper and started a slow tour of the town.

At the Longbranch, Joe Gaines asked him to talk to three

76

outriders from a cattle outfit passing close to Yellowrock. The three men were causing trouble, looking for a fight, Gaines told him. The men he pointed out were drinking at a table in the rear, shooting sullen glances at the barman and Cash.

At their table Cash nodded affably and said, 'I hear you boys are having quite a time.'

'I've had better,' one of them grunted.

'This town used to be okay till they got the law here,' another said. 'Used to be able to throw away your money and have a good spree. Now all you can do is throw away your money.'

'That's right,' Cash said. 'You can feel free to spend all the money you want.'

The third member of the trio said, 'Nobody asked you to butt in on our table. That star don't give you no right to push in where you ain't wanted.'

'That's just where I usually push in,' Cash said. 'The more I'm not wanted the more I like it. Now let's have no more tough talk. You boys just behave yourselves, and –'

The bottle swinging suddenly up into Cash's vision slashed by as he ducked his head to one side. He dodged a fist and brought his knee up under the table, scattering two men to the floor. The bottle wielder had sprung up, cat-like, as the table crashed over. Now he lunged again, the heavy glass sweeping down from above in a long powerful swing. Cash pivoted to one side as the man swept by him. Then he brought his gun down on the head that brushed his chest and turned to cover the other two.

'I think we'll take a walk,' he said quietly.

A few minutes later he marched them into the jailhouse.

'I ever get another chance at you, you'll live just long enough to be sorry for this,' the bottle wielder snarled.

'Hell,' Cash laughed. 'You talk too mean to be a fighting man.'

It was ten o'clock when Cash stepped out of the jail door and started to make another round of the town.

He had gone only a few paces when a woman's shrill voice, tense with worry, called 'Sheriff!' from up the street. A moment later a panting woman came quickly to where

77

he stood. 'You've got to help me!'

'What's the trouble, lady?'

'My little girl. She's lost. She's out wandering the hills, most likely. She hasn't been home all day and it's five hours past eating time.'

'What's her name? How old is she? What's she look like?'

'She's Jane. Jane Bowen. She's six. She's got black hair and blue eyes and two front teeth are missing.'

'What's she wearing?'

'A blue dress with a white collar.'

'Have you passed the word among your friends?'

'We don't have any friends. Jed, my husband, just got a job at the mine. We got in town only a few days ago. I been searching by myself.'

'I'll have a look around. You go down to Front Street, turn left and go to the first street you come to. That'll be Allen Street. There's a church on Allen. Man by the name of Williams runs it. He'll help you. This'll be just his meat.'

When Mrs. Bowen hurried away, Cash left the front of the jail and went back to the Longbranch. He told Joe Gaines what had happened and Joe stood up on his bar and yelled to get attention. 'I don't want to make a speech at you,' he said, 'but a six-year-old girl name of Jane Bowen is lost. The sheriff'll tell you about it.'

Cash described the girl. Then he said, 'Those of you who want to come out and look for her will be doing the kid and her mother a big favour. If you don't look, at least tell everyone you run into that she's lost. Spread the news.' He hesitated, then added, 'The man who does find her can get roaring drunk for a week – on me – without worrying about being locked up. I'll be riding out in about ten minutes.'

He was surprised that more than half of the men in the saloon were heading to the door as he went out.

Cash went through the same routine at the Oriental and Whitey's Alamo. Then he went to the stable, saddled Gold, and rode out to Front Street.

There were fifteen or twenty men on horseback already waiting for him. He told one man to wait until the next group was made up and to fan them out to the east. If still others were willing to hunt, they were to go south and north. He and his original crew would go west.

Once out of town the men broke out into a huge fan within calling distance of each other and rode slowly through the darkness. By midnight they were four miles out of town. It was cloudy and the moon stayed hidden behind a sky-wide mass of clouds to the south. Cash began to worry about how far to take the men. It seemed senseless to travel west all night. He reined over to the man next to him and said, 'You got any kids?'

'Seven.'

'Tell me. How the hell far could a six-year-old kid get inside of six or eight hours, say?'

'Depends. Some might get only to the back door. Some might be halfway to Frisco.'

'She could have gone four or five miles then?'

'Hoppin' on one leg. No trouble.'

After fifteen minutes Cash heard the wolves. Their howls came from far away, up where the sloping mountains pushed high toward a fistful of stars sprinkled near the clouds. It was a high, hunting yelp he heard first, a call for reinforcements. Then it caught a lower, baying quality that signaled it was on the trail, nose to the ground, loping tirelessly and swiftly toward its prey.

Cash wondered if the prey might be Jane Bowen. He could sense that the man riding next to him was wondering too. 'Let's ride those wolves down,' he yelled.

His companion stood in the stirrups and bellowed at the top of his voice. The men down along the line picked up the signal and understood the urgent note in it. Within a few seconds they were riding in a long, galloping line toward the eerie animal cries, answering with ear-splitting screams of their own.

In the din Cash could at first make out new voices entering the wolf pack. Then their voices disappeared and he knew the rangy, sharp-fanged criminals were at last in full flight away from the onrushing men.

Within half a minute a gun barked three times from far down the line to the left. Cash reined around and cantered toward the shots. The moon broke out from the clouds now and he could see a rider swinging down from his horse. It must be the girl. His jaw tightened as he realized what a wolf pack could do to any unarmed human, let alone a little girl, in a matter of a few snarling, tearing seconds. Then he was whirling down from his horse too.

Jane Bowen was not hurt. She looked about her with wide, frightened eyes and said, 'I'm scared!'

'Don't worry,' the man holding her said. 'They won't hurt you.'

'Who?' she asked. Then, accusingly, 'You scared me! I saw two doggies comin' up. And all of you scared 'em away. And you scared me, too!'

The man who had been first to her said, 'We're sorry. Now you just come along with us.'

Once held in front of him on the horse she said, 'I can't go with you. I got to get home.'

'This is the way home.'

She was still unconvinced. Later, when the man's arms were tired, Cash took the Bowen girl. She turned completely wide-awake eyes toward him. 'You sure this is the way home?' she demanded.

'Pretty sure.'

Then she was asleep. She was still asleep when the tired party rode back into town. Cash told the man who had found her, 'You run up the bill for a week's good time at the Longbranch. Gaines will send the bill along to me.'

'Thanks, but forget it,' the man said. 'I got myself a sprout back in Tennessee about her size.'

Cash pulled up and told the riders around him, 'This man won't take my offer. So why don't the lot of you hoist a few in the Longbranch by way of reward? Now that we've found the girl, I've got to go find her mother.'

Mrs. Bowen was waiting at the jail. She gave a cry of delight when she saw her daughter, and took her into her arms. 'You were all so wonderful,' she said, crying as she rocked the child tenderly. 'I just didn't know what to do. But you and Mr. Williams knew exactly what to do. It was wonderful.'

'I'm glad we found her,' Cash said, groping uncomfortably for words.

'I don't suppose I can explain how grateful I am. But if you took all the money and gold in the world and piled it in a big pile, we'd rather have Janey.'

'Yes, ma'am.'

'After some lucky girl catches you and you have your own, then you'll know what I mean.'

'Yes, ma'am,' Cash repeated, distinctly embarrassed. 'She must be pretty tired. Why don't you take her on home? I'll wait here at the office to tell the others she's all right.'

'God bless you.' Mrs. Bowen ducked out the door, cradling the child in her arms, and Cash sat down at the desk.

A loud, whiningly sweet voice drifted in from the cells at the back. 'Dearie me. God bless you, Sheriff. You were just wonderful!'

'Quiet down,' Cash called back.

'But Sheriff, I just wanted to say God bless –'

There was the sharp sound of knuckles meeting flesh and bone. Then another sound like the falling of a body.

Cash took the lamp and went to the cell in the back. One of his three prisoners was stretched out on the floor. The man who had tried to break the bottle over Cash's head earlier in the evening stood looking down at the fallen man, rubbing his fist gently.

'What's going on?' Cash demanded.

'You did okay, Sheriff,' the bottle fighter said simply. 'It was nice of you to go out and find that lady's baby and I ain't gonna let no drunken son make fun of it.'

'How many kids you got?' Cash asked dryly.

'I ain't got none. It's just the damned principle of it, that's all.'

81

CHAPTER SEVEN

At five-fifteen Friday evening, Cash walked down to the lobby of the Holiday Hotel.

'My, Mr. Jefferson,' the clerk said. 'You're looking particularly fine. First time I've seen you with a jacket and tie.'

Cash picked up the surrey he'd rented. Several people waved or called to him as he drove down Front Street and out toward Spangle Valley. At two minutes before seven, the surrey's wheels bumped over the rough dirt trail into Virginia's ranch yard.

Hank was sitting on the front porch. 'Hi,' he called, running to the surrey.

'What's your hair slicked down for? You coming along?'

'Nah. I've got to stay over with Jake Reny. Ma'll be out in fifteen minutes, she says. Want to come look at Lightning? Something's wrong with his hoof.'

They walked back to the stable and in the stall Cash bent over the sorrel's rear leg. He finally found a small, square-cut nail nearly out of sight in the hoof. While he was pulling it, Hank said, 'You sure know how to look a horse over. You've worked with horses a lot, I bet.'

'Some. This was deep. We'll heat a little tar and stick it on for protection.'

There was a bucket of tar in the corner of the barn. Piled high on a shelf above it were several bales of barbed wire. Leaning against the wall was a stack of iron fenceposts with sharpened points to be driven into the ground.

'Looks like there's some fencing to do,' Cash said.

'Yeah,' Hank sighed. 'We want to fence off some pasture, but the work's too tough for Ma and me all by ourselves.'

While Cash warmed the soft black mass on the end of a stick over a small fire behind the stable, Hank went at his subject again. 'What I mean is you can tell a lot about a man by little things. Ain't that so? My dad told me that.'

Cash gazed at Hank over the fire. 'What are you getting at?'

The boy was embarrassed. He said, 'Oh, I guess it doesn't matter. But it's been in my mind. I saw a fellow's eyes once, and I knew just by that – lookin' at his eyes – that he wasn't scared of nothin'. Not that they were mean. They wasn't at all. But you just knew there wasn't anything in this world had him buffaloed.'

'There are men like that. Lead that sorrel out here now, will you? And hold his halter tight.'

While Cash put the tar over the tiny hole in the hoof, Hank continued, determined to get the story out. 'Anyway, I didn't notice it so much at first, but last time you were here I did. You got eyes almost exactly like that other man's. The same kind of look to 'em.'

Cash held the horse's leg while the tar cooled, saying, 'That's interesting. Do I know the man?'

'Nope.' Hank was silent for a moment. 'He was that other fellow they were gonna have be sheriff. Mr. Sullivan.'

In the failing light Cash looked keenly at the boy. Hank gazed back at him serenely. 'That's the look. Dead ringer.'

Virginia was waiting when they walked back to the house. She wore a full white jersey gown that held softly to her slender figure. A red velvet cloak was over her shoulders, and at her throat was a dainty oval broach. Her long red hair spilled down over the cloak in curving waves.

'Good evening,' Cash said. 'Hank put me to work.'

She smiled. 'If he had his way we'd build another room onto the cabin for you to live in. There's a basin of hot water inside for you to wash in.'

When they'd left Hank at the Reny cabin and started away in the surrey, Cash said, 'It certainly has been warm lately.'

'Yes.' After a long silence, she went on. 'People are strange. I wonder how many people have talked about the weather while they were thinking a thousand other thoughts.'

'It's probably helped a lot.' Cash let the guiding tension go out of the reins and allowed the horse to pick its own way along the dark road. 'People like me might not know what to say, so we say something about the weather. I might say I generally don't like snow, but I do like to sit by

83

a fireplace when it's snowing outside. And maybe you'd say you like that too. Then I say, well we'll have to do that together some time. And there's no telling where you can go from there.'

Cash flicked the buggy whip over the ears of the mare in harness and she complained with a throaty snort.

'Another funny thing about talking. People skirt around the truth like a colt chasing a tumbleweed in the wind. I guess we're afraid of it. When I talk to you about sitting in front of a fireplace, what I really mean is that I like being with you. I'd like to be with you more.'

Virginia looked ahead and said nothing, but Cash saw that she was smiling quietly in the moonlight. . . .

Clymer's big house was set on a hill at the north side of town. Surreys and buckboards could be seen by the light streaming from its windows, and laughter and talk and music spilled out along with the light.

Clem and his wife stood near the doorway with Bill Grayson and a dark-haired girl with shining eyes whom Clymer introduced as Harriet Borland.

Hap Borland joined the group and nodded coldly to Cash. 'Do you find Yellowrock a harder or easier town to keep the law in than El Paso, Sheriff?' he asked.

Cash noticed uneasily that the man who'd lied to get him his job – the one man outside Whitey's gang who could expose him – was drunk. 'About the same,' he said. 'Wouldn't you say so, having been in El Paso at the same time?'

The mild reminder disturbed Borland. 'I'd say Yellowrock was worse,' he muttered. 'Got to have another drink. Isn't every day a man's daughter lands a fine young man like Bill Grayson.'

'You've got it backwards,' Grayson said from where he stood with Harriet in the circled group. 'It isn't every day a man like me lands a girl like your daughter.'

Cash said, 'It seems to me as a sporting man that marriage is the only gamble in which both players can win.'

There was a rippled of pleased laughter and friendly agreement. Cash took Virginia through the crowd to the punch bowl. While he was filling her glass, she opened her eyes wide and said in mock admiration, 'Why, Mr. Jefferson, you're actually clever with words. You must have taken a mail-order course.'

Cash handed her the glass and took one for himself. 'Every now and then my genius just bubbles out. There's no holding it down.'

Williams appeared out of a group near the centre of the room and made his way to where they were. 'Sheriff, if I could erase a quarter of a century from my age, you would be hard to put to keep this young lady through the evening.'

Virginia favoured him with a radiant smile. 'Using that sort of flattery, you should have your church filled to overflowing in no time.'

'Everything a minister says is suspect,' Williams sighed. 'Yet it's true that I have always been partial to redheads.'

'Will you be performing the ceremony?' she asked.

'Yes. I wish more young couples around here would get married so I could get back in practice.'

There was a tense pause in their conversation while Williams folded his hands behind his back and stared with grave interest at the crystal chandelier hanging from the ceiling.

Harriet Borland broke the silence by crossing the room and saying, 'Would you gentlemen mind if I take Virginia away for a moment?'

When they'd moved away, talking eagerly together, Cash said, 'Well, Preacher, how are things going? You figure the town's soul is improving?'

'The town's in a bad way now. But I'm certain good things are coming. I can smell them like rain on the wind.'

'I don't see much wrong with the way things are.'

Williams said in a low, suddenly sharp voice. 'Have you been paying much attention to the south side of town?'

'No call to. No trouble there. Things are usually quiet.'

'Naturally. The people who live there go up to Front Street to fight and drink and get into trouble. But you know mining towns well enough to know that that's where the people freeze to death in whole families in the winter. That's where rats gnaw at the unclaimed corpses before they're shoveled, half a dozen at a time, into the nearest hole. That's where the children – the lucky ones – grow up hungry and mean, ready to cut a throat for a square meal, or completely beaten and hopeless.'

'You can't stop that kind of thing.'

'You can't if no one tries,' Williams agreed. 'But you could if there was someone strong enough to do a little amputating.'

'And what would you amputate, Doctor?'

'You ever hear of a man named Whitey Hall?'

Cash stopped grinning. 'Sure.'

'I know that he's a hard man. How hard I don't know. He controls the saloons and gambling halls and the dear Lord knows what all. He's done more than anyone else to cause the rotten state of affairs in Yellowrock.'

'Maybe you could convert him.'

'He seems to be too powerful to convince in any other way. If you tried force it's my guess you'd need the United States Army. I'll have to try to make him see his errors.'

'Good luck.'

Virginia came up then and took Cash by the elbow and smiled at the preacher. 'May I borrow Mr. Jefferson? They're starting to dance in the next room and I need a partner.'

Driving Virginia home under the broad arch of star-studded sky, Cash was happy to find that conversation was not necessary. The silence was warm, and they were closer together with no words between them.

At last he said, 'Did you have a good time?'

'Yes. Did you?'

'Terrible.'

He felt her large eyes swing to him. 'Why?'

'Too many people. It would have been better if there had been – oh, say, you and me, and that's all.'

'We can have our own party. Let's pretend that I have a magic wand and that I can touch you with it like this!' She brushed the back of his hand with her fingertip. 'And now I can tell everything you're thinking!'

'This may lead to trouble.'

She laughed. 'Then I'll tell you what I think of you. First, I think you think you're extremely strong and able.'

'True, of course.'

'I think there are a few men in Yellowrock who are homelier than you.'

'Poor devils.'

'Also, I think there's a part of you missing. At times I think I understand you. Then, at other times, I know I don't.'

'Us deep fellows are tough to understand.'

'What do you think of me?'

Cash stared at a large star tipping a peak in the distance. 'I think what everyone else does. You're pretty and nice to be with. Somehow, too, you put me in mind of the tinkle of sleighbells.'

'That's a pretty compliment.' She leaned back against the leather seat. After a time, she said, 'Why so quiet?'

'I'm wondering about Williams, Clymer, Grayson, Joe Gaines. Wondering how they feel about me.'

'They like you, I'm sure. I know they respect you.'

'They shouldn't.'

She sat up straight. 'That's an odd things to say.'

'In my game it doesn't pay to get close to people.'

'You sound stranger all the time. What do you mean?'

Cash struggled for an evasive answer. 'Sheriffs are made to get shot at.'

After Cash pulled the mare to a halt in front of Virginia's home he twisted the reins around the dashboard peg and helped her from the surrey.

At the doorway she turned and said, 'I've been doing some thinking myself.'

'What?'

Her voice became a whisper and she put her hands on his arms. 'In some ways I don't like your being sheriff. I know that if I ever get – close to you, sometimes I'd be afraid. But it would be all right, because I'd always be able to be proud of you.'

The muscles in Cash's arms stiffened and she looked up to see his jaw set tight in the moonlight. 'What's the matter?'

'Nothing.' His voice was hard.

'This is the part of you I don't understand. I haven't seen it so clearly before.' She released his arms and stepped back. 'There's something about you that's all wrong.'

'How many people do you know who are perfect?' Cash demanded angrily.

'Good night.' She went in and shut the door firmly. Cash strode to the surrey and leaped into the seat. Its whirling wheels scattered small rocks as it rolled swiftly into the night. . . .

On his way to the jail at seven o'clock the next morning Cash met Whitey and Duke coming out of the barbershop down the street from the Alamo. 'Morning,' he said.

'Hello, Sheriff,' Hall greeted him. 'Been meaning to have a word with you.' He lowered his voice. 'Smart work the way you got that kid back to her old lady. The way things go, the time may come when we'll have to stage an election for city officials. Public feeling the way it is right now, you'd win in a walk.'

'I try to keep everybody happy.'

'But I've got a new thorn in my side. That preacher Williams came by.'

'So early?'

'He must get up in the middle of the night. And he must have been chewing loco weed. He asked me for a donation to help build a school.'

'He's a little touched all right.'

'I've been going to get around to booting him out of town, but haven't had the time. I think I'll throw a scare into him.'

'I'd go easy on him,' Cash said. 'He seems harmless.'

'Don't forget Ben,' Duke said.

'Oh, yes. Ben got into a ruckus last night. Broke a Mexican's back. If the spic's family tries to cause any trouble give them a song and dance and toss them out.'

'Okay, Whitey.'

'Why you got such polite manners this mornin'?' Duke asked.

'I want to get in good with Whitey so I can take over your spot when a medium-sized wind blows you out of town.'

Duke's lips moved to an angle that might have been a grin. 'Thought you might be too damned pooped to argue, after seein' that redhead woman home last night.'

'Stop it Duke,' Whitey said.

'No damage,' Cash said easily, though his heart was

pounding. 'As I told you before, my only loyalty is to Cash.'

At his office he decided he wanted a smoke and began rummaging through his desk looking for some cigars he'd put there.

He found them and was striking a match to one when a young Mexican girl came in. Her eyes were red and her face lined from crying, but she spoke calmly. 'I try to find you last night. My husban' was murdered. His name Raphael Pinaro.'

'Oh,' Cash said. 'Sit down. I heard about that.'

She remained standing. 'From who?'

'Couple of men I talked to this morning.'

'They lie. I know they lie. All men in this town are afraid of the man who do it. Name of Ben. I don' know his last name.'

'They tell me it was self-defense.'

The girl's fists clenched and unclenched but her voice remained calm, almost monotonous in tone. 'You see this?' She ran her hand down the complete length of her dress where it had been torn and crudely pinned back together. 'Ben was drunk. He came into where we live. I was alone. He tore my dress off. He threw me down. We were on the floor when my husban' come home. He try to help me. Ben kill him in this way – he, he break him over his knee.'

'Your husband attacked Ben. Tried to kill him.'

'This is the law?' she asked in a tiny voice.

She came to the desk and leaned over it, her eyes wide. Suddenly she pounded the desk and shouted, 'This is the law?' She repeated the words over and over, beating the desk until she collapsed over it, panting like a wounded animal.

Cash took a bottle from a shelf on the wall and poured a shot of whisky. 'Maybe this will make you feel better.' He placed it on the desk before the sobbing girl.

She stood up and forced her crying back into her chest. She picked up the glass abruptly and tossed the whisky into his face. Then she ran out of the jail. . . .

In the afternoon Williams came into the office. 'A little Mexican girl named Carmen Pinaro came to see you this morning.'

'Yes.'

'A friend brought her to see me. The girl's in a bad way.

She was almost murdered – as well as her husband.'

'Those girls all have the same story, Williams. They'll go along with an offer of four bits and then yell bloody murder if their husband catches them.'

Williams said harshly, 'You don't believe that happened to this girl! You can't believe it!'

'I do believe it. Naturally the girl's upset, but she –'

'Stop it, Cash,' Williams said. 'You saved a little girl from wolves not long ago. How would you have felt if the wolves had got there first?'

'What's that got to do with it?'

'The animals got to this girl! You know it, and I know it. We know what happened to her husband. How can you stand there and argue about it? I'm swearing out a warrant for the arrest of the maniac who did it right now.' He added bitterly, 'This is where you swear out warrants, isn't it?'

'Swear a warrant if you want. But there are witnesses who saw the girl making up to Ben before the fight.'

'I see. How could he know her husband wouldn't approve? All he did was defend himself when the man tried to kill him?'

'That's right.'

'You're protecting Ben. Ben works for Whitey Hall. It adds up very quick and easy, doesn't it?'

'I don't know what you're talking about, Williams. I'm not protecting anyone – unless they happen to be innocent of what they're charged with.'

Williams took off his hat and wiped sweat from the inside band. 'I'm sorry.'

'For what?'

'I'm truly sorry. Perhaps when we get older our sight fails us. I believed I saw in you something that wasn't there. You're no different from Whitey or his two bodyguards, or those other three vultures sitting on a fence. You're the same as they are.'

'I still don't know what you're talking about.'

'Yes you do. Don't worry. I can't prove it. But I know you're working for Hall.'

'You'd better not spread a rumour like that. It would be damned dangerous.'

'I won't. Without evidence I'd just be an old man talking to himself. But I'm sorry I misjudged you. It takes something out of me and out of my work here.'

'In that case it might not be a bad idea to get out and go someplace else.'

'No, I can't do that. I'll just go on trying.' He looked old and tired standing near the doorway with his hat in his hand.

Cash took the bottle from the shelf again and poured a shot. 'I'm sorry about what happened to that girl and her husband. But it's done. You can't go back and undo it. Drink?'

'No. I won't drink with you.'

Cash tossed it off himself and put the empty glass down roughly on the desk. 'Williams, there're some things a man can't change. One of them is the way he is.'

'Some men can. I knew that once you put on that badge you'd get a taste of new and different things, things like being looked up to, being respected. I believed you'd gradually begin to appreciate the wonder of helping other people, that you'd learn the value of pride and human dignity. But I'm talking like a preacher again.'

'I promise you this, Williams. I won't do anything to anybody that hasn't been tried on me. I couldn't.'

Williams put his hat on and said quietly, 'I'll send that Pinaro girl back to her folks in Los Angeles. I'm sorry for you, Cash.'

When Williams had gone, Cash sat at his desk and leaned his forehead against the knuckle of his left fist. After a few minutes he took an envelope from a drawer. He put two hundred dollars in the envelope and sealed it carefully.

He found Ma Bracken at her restaurant and gave her the envelope. 'Look, Ma. You know the little Pinaro girl? She's the one – '

'Yeah. I know her.'

'Well, give her this, will you?'

Ma Bracken held the envelope up to the light from the window. 'Money. You buyin' off a sore conscience?'

'Nothing like that,' Cash mumbled. 'It's just – maybe it'll help her some.'

Ma stuck the envelope into her apron pocket. 'I'll give it to her.'

CHAPTER EIGHT

Sunday night, Williams was pistol-whipped.

Monday morning Joe Gaines was standing in the lobby when Cash came down from his room at the Holiday.

'You hear about Williams yet?'

'No. What about him?'

'He was beat up late last night. They just found him a couple hours ago.'

'He hurt much?'

'A gun barrel laid across the face a few times was never known to do anybody any good. But he ain't serious. I patched him up. He'll be all right in a few days.'

'Did he see who did it?'

'No. He was walkin' down Allen. Dark as the ten of spades, he says. Somebody upped beside him and that's all he remembers. They dumped him behind a fence. Some kid walkin' the fence this mornin' saw him and told his old lady. She got me.'

'Where's he now?'

'In his room in back of the church. Couple of ladies are lookin' out for him. I thought I'd drop by and tell you. Funny thing, though.' Gaines glanced uncomfortably at the leather bag in his hand. 'I told him I'd tell you about it and he said don't bother. He said he didn't see who done it and there was no point in troublin' you about the whippin'. Ain't that funny?'

Cash didn't answer.

That afternoon Saul fell in with Cash as he was walking up Front Street for dinner. 'Whitey wants to see you tonight. About nine at the Alamo.'

When Cash knocked at the door to Whitey's office it edged open and Duke said, 'Come in.' The three gunmen, Saul, Garf, and Lewt were in the room with Duke and Whitey. Hall said, 'I hear that poor preacher got his head somewhat banged up.'

Cash said, 'So they tell me. Who did it?'

'Garf and Lewt here. I wish I could have done it myself, though. Soon as Williams is up and around I don't doubt he'll be leaving town.'

Garf said, 'If he don't, he'll get it worse next time.'

'I owe you an apology, Garf,' said Cash. 'I underestimated you. I didn't think you were game enough to go right up behind an old man that way and take him on with only one man helping you.'

'Quit riding him, Cash,' Hall ordered. 'He was doing what I told him to do. I don't want to hear that kind of talk. And I think it might be a good idea if you turned up the man who bent a barrel over the preacher's head. Any stray drunk you pick up will do. He'll confess and that'll be all there is to it. People will be satisfied.'

'That all?'

'Yes, all for now. But stay where I can find you.'

Cash nodded and walked out.

Next morning when Cash got to his office he found Garf waiting.

'What do you want?' Cash said sharply.

'No need to get nasty. Saul was too drunk, so Whitey told me to bring this to you.' Garf tossed an envelope on the desk. 'For all your big talk, you get paid just like the rest of us.'

After Garf sauntered out the door Clem Clymer walked in. 'I never thought I'd see that fellow come willingly within a mile of a jailhouse,' he said.

'All kinds come by.'

Clymer stared after Garf's retreating figure and Cash pushed the envelope on his desk into a drawer. 'What can I do for you?'

'Nothing,' said Clymer. 'I was just wonderin' if anything's happened between you and Virginia.'

'That's between her and me, isn't it?'

'Yes. But I'm a nosy old cuss. She was feeling bad enough lately. But then she went to visit Preacher Williams yesterday, just to wish him well. And she came back lookin' like she'd had a sunstroke – white and shaky. She told me she and him had a little talk. That's all she'd say. But I got a hunch it was about you.'

93

'Your hunch is as good as mine.'

'Maybe.' Clymer thought about it a minute. 'One thing. Plenty of folks, and Virginia, was pretty sore about that little Pinaro girl and her husband. They think you should have done more.'

'It was –'

'I know,' Clymer interrupted. 'Self-defense. That big son of a bitch claiming self-defense is like a landslide claiming self-defense.'

'Ben must be behaving himself. I haven't see him since it happened.'

'He was at my place today. Drunk. Just stood and gawked at Virginia. Then he said something she couldn't quite make out and left. She's not scared of many things, but she's scared of him.' Clymer stopped talking, then rubbed his jaw slowly. 'You got nothin' to say about that?'

'There's no law against a man going into a store and leaving without buying anything.'

'If that's the way you feel about it – ' Clymer frowned at the floor – 'that's all I got to say.'

That night Cash slept badly. The next night he didn't get a chance to sleep. At midnight he was on Front Street when he heard a shot from the outskirts of town. In a short time a man ran swiftly up the walk on the other side of the street, shouted to him and dashed over to where Cash stood.

'Sheriff!' he gasped through his heavy breathing. 'Jim Wilson's gone out of his head. Tryin' to kill his whole damned family!'

'Where?'

'Down on the south side. I'll take you. Come on!'

The man turned and sped away, Cash keeping pace at his side. A crowd had gathered around the last frame shack where Fremont Street tapered off into the wide expanse of dark prairie beyond. One man held a torch and was shouting to someone inside.

As the two ran up through the shadows to join the crowd, Cash could hear the sound of an ax ringing inside the shack.

The man with the torch said, 'Sheriff, Wilson's in there chopping down the door to the pantry. He swore he'd kill his wife and kids! They're in there!'

'Let's stop him,' said Cash, starting for the front door.

'He's got a rifle,' someone in the crowd called. 'Took a shot at me when I went in.'

The voices in the crowd were stilled as the solid thump of the swinging ax inside gave way to a splintering sound. 'He's at them!' a woman screamed.

Cash was inside the house in a few running strides. Wilson, a man he recognized as having seen often walking quietly and alone on Front Street, was crouching before the pantry door, reaching through a shattered hole in it to find the bar on the other side. Cash could hear children whimpering behind the door. Eyes wild and glazed, Wilson was so engrossed with trying to reach inside that he didn't notice Cash for a moment. When he did, he stopped all movement and glared with furious intensity.

His hand began edging toward the rifle leaning against the wall near him. He leaped for it as Cash stepped forward and brought his Colt crashing down. Wilson slumped to the floor.

A woman's voice, tense and terrified, came from within the pantry. 'Who's there?'

'The sheriff. It's all right to come out now.'

Knowing it was now safe, the neighbors outside began to flock into the Wilson home. A matronly woman put her arm around the gray-faced Mrs. Wilson and two other women scooped up the bewildered, frightened children.

A curious onlooker was sitting in a wagon drawn up before the shack. Cash and two other men dumped Wilson into the back of it. Twenty minutes later the wild man was stretched out on a cell cot, glaring vacantly into space.

Cash slept in the chair behind his desk that night. No telling what the madman would try to do.

A light knocking brought him wide awake, hands tensed over his Colts. It was morning, and early beams of light flowed through the window on the east side of his office. Mrs. Wilson stood at the door. She said, 'How is Jim?'

'Fine. He's lying down back here.'

Before his cell, she called softly, 'Jim?'

Wilson hadn't moved all night. The first time she called, her voice didn't get to him. The second time, he turned and looked at her. He didn't speak.

'It's all right, Jim,' she said. 'It's all right.'

Back in the front office she looked at Cash with tired, worried eyes. 'He'll be no more trouble, Sheriff. He won't do anything wrong. He got this way from living on the south side for two years. God knows how many times we've been close to freezing or starving in that shack. Jim's got his weaknesses. Lots of times he's tried to bring in extra money from bucking the tiger, and managed to lose what little he had, but he's always done his best for us. I mean – ' She hesitated. 'He'll be all right, now. Please. Can you let him go?'

'I'm sorry. I can't.'

'I was afraid of that. He's been worrying so terribly. I guess it was bound to come to this. I guess it's been coming for a long time. But does he have to go to jail?'

'No. There's a place up north of Grandville where they keep people like your husband.'

'I don't want that, Sheriff. There's a special home in California I know about. Things are nice there.'

'That sort of place costs money.'

'I used to be a housekeeper. There are places they'll hire me if I sign for five years. I can get some money in advance. We'll manage.'

Four days later two husky guards from the Gable Manor Home in Sacramento came to take Jim Wilson with them. They had state papers from California giving them permission to assume responsibility for the mentally deranged person. Wilson had not said a word since he'd tried to kill Cash, and he didn't speak as they drove him away to the railroad station in Grandville in an enclosed hack.

Mrs. Wilson came by the jail a few hours later. 'I want to thank you for what you did, Sheriff. The young ones and me will be taking the three o'clock stage out. We're going to San Francisco. We'll be close to Jim.'

'You're sure doing a lot for him.'

She smiled at Cash and said simply, 'Jim has always looked out for us; now I've got to look out for him.'

That night Cash saw Ben in front of the Oriental as he was making his rounds of the town. He went up to the big man and said, 'I've been wanting to see you.'

'Yeah. What for?'

'Walk along. This is just between us.'

When they were in a dark spot between buildings Cash stopped and said, 'Remember that Pinaro girl?'

'What about her?' Ben leaned threateningly close, his breath sour and hot on Cash's forehead.

'If you ever treat another girl like that, any girl, I'll kill you.'

Ben snorted. 'You tryin' to toss a scare into me?'

Cash slapped him hard with the back of his hand. Taken by surprise, Ben went back one step, caught his balance and started forward, his huge arms out-spread. He was stopped by the barrel of Cash's Colt jabbing into his stomach. 'I said I'd kill you. I mean it,' Cash whispered.

'Some time you won't have them guns on. I'll tear off your ears for keepsakes.' Ben suddenly stopped glaring and showed his uneven teeth in a slow smile. 'I know what you're thinkin' of. That redhead!'

'Walk down the street. Don't forget what I said.' Cash jammed the gun harder. 'Go on!'

Ben turned and walked away. . . .

The next night Saul stopped Cash as he was leaving his office. 'You hear about the rumpus over to Clymer's Dry Goods a couple hours ago?'

'No. What happened?'

'It was funny as hell. Whitey'll tell you about it. He wants to see you.'

'Did the girl who works there get hurt?' Cash's voice was thin.

'That cute carrot-topped gal? No. Whitey'll tell you about it. Better get over there. Gonna be a busy night. Whitey's in a hurry to see you.'

Cash circled around to the back of the Alamo. Whitey and Duke were in the office. Hall's face was set in anger. 'Shut the door!' he snapped.

'What's the trouble?'

'That dirty little preacher is the trouble. Beating him up didn't do any good. I should've got rid of him long ago. I've been too patient, too easygoing.'

'What did he do?'

'He damned near killed Ben,' said Duke. 'That's what he did. And you said we should take it easy on him.' Hall went on, 'Ben was over at Clymer's around closing time, and he got a little handy with the girl who works for Clymer. He didn't actually hurt the fool woman, but he was holding onto her and she was crying a little. That was all. And the preacher comes in and sees what's going on and picks up a wagon tongue nearby and damn near knocks Ben's head off with it.'

'What's the tragedy? Did he bust the wagon tongue?' Cash said acidly.

'Don't be making fun of Ben,' Duke snarled. 'He's still out cold because of your preacher. Took three men to drag him up to his room.'

'Both of you be quiet,' Whitey said. 'This's why you're here, Cash. In a little while Saul and Garf and Lewt are going to ride down Allen Street in front of the church. They're going to put on a big act of drunken cowhands whooping it up and shooting off their guns. They'll put a few shots into the church. In the dark, one of them will run in and put a slug through Williams. I want you to give them enough time to be sure he's dead – then get over there when the shooting's finished. You can swear it was impossible to see who was raising hell. And you can verify that Williams was accidentally shot by one of the shells going through the church.'

Cash's eyes narrowed. He said, 'Where are the three boys now?'

Hall didn't notice the slight change of expression. 'How should I know? Somewhere around town.'

Duke scowled at Cash. 'What's it matter where they are now?'

Ignoring the question, Cash told Hall, 'If they're doing it pretty quick I'd better get going.'

Outside of the Alamo he walked swiftly to Front Street and hurried along it, looking into the saloons where the three men hung out most often. The town seemed strangely silent. The bars were only half filled, making the search easy. But the men were not to be found.

A rider on a big bay trotted off Front to darkened First Street and Cash recognized Saul. 'Wait a second!' he called, running up to the horse and rider.

'Oh, it's you.' Saul put his gun back as Cash came up. 'What do you want?'

Cash said, 'Got a minute?'

'Just barely. The fellows are waitin' up at the end of Allen. Whitey told you what was up, didn't he?'

'Yes. Look, Saul. You sure you like working for Whitey?'

'Sure. You been at the bottle?'

'I know this is a lot to throw at you at once. But you said once you wanted to get out and go to Wyoming.'

'Yeah. But talk's cheap. What's got into you?'

'You're young. You can get out. Maybe make a better deal for yourself.'

'Goin' straight?'

'Yes.'

'Call it yellow if you want, but if I tried to pull out I'd get a bullet in the back. Now get outa my way. We both got jobs to do.'

'This is the last chance you'll get!'

For answer Saul dug his spurs deep into the bay and the agonized horse lunged forward, knocking Cash sprawling to the ground. Cash spun as a slug plowed into the ground near his head. Another raked his arm like a glowing coal brushed across it. Then the hoofs of Saul's horse flashed by him as Saul thundered away through the darkness.

Cash stood up. His left arm was useless. There was no feeling in it. He ran toward the church on Allen Street.

Cutting through the field and behind the jail, he heard loud shouts and the wild blasts of guns. He got to the church as the gunmen put a few crashing shots into the building. He ducked through a side door as the roar of a gun fired inside the main entrance echoed hard against his ears. Williams was only fifteen feet away. His small body was flung back by the force of the slug. A second bullet tore into the wall above Cash as he dropped to one knee and pulled his Colt. He could hear the sound of running steps, but could see no one in the shadowed church. Then, for a split second, the outline of a man was visible as he went out the door. Cash threw a quick shot and the man pitched his hands up and toppled down the stairs.

There was a brief shouting outside, then the sound of horses racing away.

Cash knelt beside Williams in the dark. He was surprised when the preacher's firm voice came up to him. 'Did the leopard change its spots?'

'You hurt much?'

'Don't know. Can't feel a thing.'

Cash's left arm was beginning to burn with pain but he could now control the muscles. 'I'll take you down to Joe Gaines.'

He picked the little man up in his arms and carried him out of the church. At the front step he saw a body lying face down. The blood flowing unhurriedly from the hole in the man's back looked like mud in the moonlight. He turned the body over with his foot. It was Lewt.

At the Longbranch the few men in the bar clustered around as Cash walked in with Williams. Joe Gaines walked over swiftly, glanced at the preacher and said, 'In the back room.' There Cash laid him down on a couch.

Williams was hit in one side of the chest. Going over the wound, Gaines said, 'It's bad. Depends what sets in later. Who did it?'

'Killers hired by Whitey Hall,' Williams muttered. 'Jefferson chased them away.'

'Got to get my kit from behind the bar,' Gaines said. 'Don't move, Williams.' He went out the door.

'I heard what you did for Virginia today,' Cash said. 'Always admired a man who'd tackle somebody Ben's size.'

'That little incident wasn't all it took to turn you around. There was a lot of thinking building up to that.' Williams coughed and spit blood. 'Believe me, the town will be behind you. You'll have all the help you need cleaning up.'

'I'm not looking for help.'

'But Hall's got a fair-sized army behind him.' Williams choked and more blood trailed from his lips.

'He's got plenty of errand boys around town. But only four dangerous men. Garf and Saul, and Ben and Duke.'

'That makes five with Whitey himself. You tackle them alone and you're a dead man.'

'That's the way it's got to be.'

Williams noticed Cash's arm for the first time. The shirt was torn, the arm bleeding. 'You're hurt.'

'Not much. Not nearly as much as you are after playing sheriff at Clymer's today.'

'I played sheriff because we didn't have one in town. I'll never try a stunt like that again – now that we have got a sheriff.'

CHAPTER NINE

Gaines came into the room and locked the door behind him. 'Saul and Garf were out front just now. They asked me if I'd seen you. From their faces they was bent on killin'.'

'What did you tell them?'

'I told 'em I hadn't seen nothin'. They missed the blood on the floor. And the men that was out there didn't let on neither.'

'Williams is in danger. Can you keep him here for a while?'

'Sure. But they didn't give a damn about Williams. It was you they were after.'

'This young fool,' Williams gasped, 'plans to take on Hall and his men singlehanded.' His breathing was becoming heavy and strained. He closed his eyes. His breathing seemed to stop.

Cash moved forward. 'Is he dead?'

'No. But he may be before morning. Hold that lamp closer. . . .'

Much later Gaines stepped away. He rolled his sleeves down and sighed. 'There's one preacher that sure as hell is in the hands of God.'

'Thanks, Joe. I'll be moving on now.'

'Wait.' Gaines put out a restraining hand. 'Williams is right. You can't fight Hall alone. Get the people behind you. Even up the odds.'

'Get who behind me? Clymer? Borland? Grayson? You, Joe?'

'Well maybe none of us is much with a gun, but there's officers up to Grandville and —'

'You can count on just one man in a showdown. Yourself. Besides, this is a personal fight.'

'Wait till I fix that arm, anyway.'

'No time. I've got to talk to someone before the shooting starts.'

Cash got to the stable without being seen. He picked his saddle up and threw it over Gold, then swung aboard and

102

started out of town. He squeezed Gold into a long lope and headed toward Spangle Valley. Gold went down a steep hill in rough, stiff-legged leaps and Cash felt his shoulder wound tear open again. Soon he could feel warm blood trickling down his arm.

It was almost daylight when he swung Gold up the slight incline before Virginia's house. A light, hollow dizziness spun through his head as he stood in the stirrups and dropped to the ground. He walked to the porch and knocked at the door.

Virginia's voice came from the corner of the house. 'Raise your hands over your head!'

He turned to see her fully dressed, holding a rifle on him in a steady, businesslike manner. 'Up!' she commanded. 'You're not the only one around here who can use a gun.'

Cash tried to grin and it didn't quite come off. 'Everyone's pointing guns at me these days.'

'I'm ready to do more than point,' she said in a husky voice. 'I've shot two Mescaleros off that porch.'

Cash started to speak and the dizziness came back worse than before. A tiny speck of blackness grew in the middle of his mind until it at last obliterated everything else. He fell down on the wooden planks of the porch.

'Get up!' Virginia snapped. 'Don't try tricks on me!'

She walked nearer and noticed his shirt sleeve soaked with blood. She dropped the gun and knelt beside him. 'Cash. Cash! Hank, come out here!'

When Cash fought his way back through the darkness he was on the bunk in the cabin and the rising sun was glinting through the window near the fireplace. Hank was seated in a chair a few feet away watching him. Virginia was working over the stove.

'He's awake, Ma,' Hank announced.

Virginia turned around. She said coldly, 'How's your shoulder?'

Cash looked down toward the bullet wound. It was bandaged neatly and his arm felt good, almost strong. 'Fine. Thanks for doctoring it.'

'Don't thank me. It was Hank's idea.'

Something about what Cash had seen when he looked down caused him to twist his neck once more and frown at the expanse of shirt and bandage. Then he realized what it was. His badge was gone.

Hank's careful, sober eyes never left him. He said, 'I took it.'

Virginia stood near her son. In her delicate hand one of Cash's Colts looked absurdly oversized. 'If you're feeling all right, you can get up and ride out of here.'

'I came in to talk to you.'

'I talked to Williams. That's enough. I should have known what you were as soon as Hank told me who came to town with you on the stage.'

Cash sat up slowly and put his feet on the floor. 'That's what I came to talk to you about.'

'Is it true what she says?' Hank asked slowly. 'Were you laughin' at me when I give you that badge? Ain't you a real sheriff?'

'I'm trying to be, Hank. And I wouldn't laugh at you. You know that.'

'Ma and me worked up a lot of feelin' for Preacher Williams. And he told her – '

'He told me you were a wonderful man,' Virginia said bitterly. 'But that you just happened to be hired out to the crooks who run Yellowrock. He wanted me to try to talk you into respecting yourself and your job. But self-respect has got to come from inside. And you obviously haven't got it.'

Cash shrugged his shoulders and winced. 'I came out here to tell you about that. I'm sorry about the way things were. I'm trying to make it up.'

Hank stood. 'I believe him. I like him. I know what he does will be right!' He ran from the room.

Cash shifted slightly forward on the bunk and Virginia cocked the Colt. He looked up in surprise at the dry, deadly click. His lips tightened. 'Why don't you pull the trigger and be done with it?'

'I will, if you make another move.'

'Get ready to shoot then,' Cash said angrily. He got to his feet and stared down at Virginia. Her face was pale. Then gun was steady, but she did not fire.

He walked to the window and looked out at the trail leading toward Yellowrock. It was deserted. 'If it will make

104

you any happier, chances are good I'll be dead within twenty-four hours. Before it happens, I want to tell you a couple of things about myself.'

'Why should you be dead within twenty-four hours?' Her voice was tiny, almost a whisper.

'Because I've broken with Hall.' He grinned. 'You don't think my shoulder got hurt playing mumblety-peg, do you?'

'Don't joke if you're in danger.' She lowered the revolver. 'How did you get hurt?'

'One of Hall's men took a shot at me. Worse than that, Williams was shot in the chest. He may have died by now. It's my fault. If I'd moved faster, if I'd gone straight to him, I might have stopped it.' Cash rubbed his hand through his hair. 'Up to last night I was on Hall's payroll. Then – I don't know, when they decided to kill Williams I couldn't go through with it. Ever since they made me sheriff, I've found myself wanting to be what I was supposed to be. Things I never thought of before have been building up somewhere in the back of my head. I can't explain them. But they boiled over last night.'

'Why did you ride out here? Why did you want to talk to me?'

'I'm not sure. I know I wanted to straighten out two things. One, the first time I came out here Whitey thought Sullivan might have talked to Hank – I was sent out to kill him.'

Virginia's lips parted and she stopped breathing to stare up at him with disbelief. Then she took a deep breath and said, 'Could you have done such a thing? Could you have killed a little boy?'

'I don't know. I never will. I know I couldn't now.'

She shut her eyes for a moment. 'Neither of us must ever speak of that again.' She opened them and looked back at him. 'What was the other thing?'

'To say that I'm sorry for our argument the night I took you to Clymer's party. You said there was something missing in me. There was. I was a coward. Afraid to stick up for things, afraid of any responsibility except my own hide. Maybe I'm still a coward. I'm scared stiff. But for the first time that I can remember, I'm willing to fight for what I

105

know is right.' Cash worked the muscles in his hurt arm and flexed his fingers. 'I've been talking too much. Arm feels pretty good now.'

Virginia walked to the far side of the room. She was half laughing, half crying, the Colt held loosely in her hand. 'And now you're going to get yourself killed because you think that's the right thing to do?'

'There's no middle ground. Either you fight or you don't fight. Seems to me if you half fight, it's no fight at all.'

'But you don't do it all by yourself. That's ridiculous.'

'Maybe.'

Virginia looked at his face, the firm jaw and unwavering eyes, and waited for him to continue speaking, but he said nothing. She went to the cupboard. From it she took his second Colt and handed his guns to him. He released the cocked hammer of the one and slipped them into his holsters.

'Next time you pass out around here,' she said, 'I promise not to swipe your guns.'

'It's become something of a bad habit.'

'Before you go you've got to eat something. You've lost a lot of blood. The Indians say steak is the best medicine for anything but a toothache.'

Virginia cooked while Cash stationed himself at the window to watch the trail. He asked, 'Why were you up so early, with a Winchester in your hand at that?'

'Today's a working day, so I had to get up early. I saw you coming. I didn't know you were on our side now.'

'I'm glad you believe me. I was afraid you might not.'

She went to the fireplace for a pinch of salt and turning said, 'I'm sure you didn't get that nick in your arm playing mumblety-peg.'

'Is that the only reason you believe me?'

'No. There are better reasons.' She hesitated. 'Maybe we can talk about them another time.'

Cash tried to sound confident. He said, 'I'll hold you to that. We'll talk another time.'

Later, on the porch, Virginia put her hand on his arm. 'If I were a man like you, in your position, I think I'd have to do what you're doing. But please, Cash, come back.'

'Better stay out of town, Virginia.'

'All right.' She stretched up and kissed him.

Cash lifted himself lightly into the saddle and rode away. Virginia watched him go, then went back into the house and lay on her face on the bunk, crying.

He swung Gold back onto the trail and pushed the stallion into a long lope.

At the outskirts of Yellowrock he slowed to a walk and moved through empty streets, his busy eyes sweeping every detail around him. Most places of business were closed and locked, with shutters pulled over the windows. The bars were open, but no noise came from them.

At the Longbranch he got down from Gold and walked in. Joe Gaines was behind the bar. Two miners sat at a table in the back of the room.

'Cash!' Joe moved down the bar to him and lowered his voice. 'They've been lookin' everywhere for you.'

'How's Williams?'

'Unconscious, still. Touch and go.'

'Where is everybody?'

'Hidin', for God's sakes. Word's got around that Hall was behind the Williams shooting and that you stopped it. People expect a big blowup. Hall hasn't showed, and he's keepin' Duke with him for protection. But Ben and Saul and Garf were roamin' around the streets all mornin'. Then, for some reason, Saul and Garf lit out toward the mines about half an hour ago. They must think you're out there.'

'Yeah.' He turned from the bar.

'Cash.'

'What?' He stopped and looked back.

'It's out in the open now. Folks know about Hall and his crew. That's about all one man ought to have to do. You've done enough by yourself.'

'Thanks for the thought, Joe.' Cash went back out and swung onto Gold. A few minutes later he was taking a short cut to the mines.

At the rocky ridge above the mines he saw them, two pin-sized men on antlike horses far away and below. They were riding slowly toward the scattered buildings around the Lucky Bronco shaft. Cash reined toward a long finger of forest a short distance down the slope and rode downhill behind the protection of trees. He tied Gold in a thicket a few hundred yards from the mining camp and made his way on foot to the edge of the trees that surrounded the camp.

Garf was sitting his pony near the shaft, turning his head from side to side, searching the buildings around him carefully. Saul was riding toward a miner who stood near a well only a few feet from the fringe of trees. The young gunman drew his horse to a halt near the well. Cash could hear him plainly when he spoke.

'Hey, you. Where's all the others at? How come they ain't nobody in sight around here?'

'It's noon. They're all up to the chuckhouse.' The miner pointed at a long building at the far edge of the clearing.

'You seen that sheriff, Jefferson?'

'Nope. Can't say I have.'

'Get back to the chuckhouse with the others. Tell 'em that the first man who sticks his head out of there gets it blown off. Savvy?'

'You bet!' The man picked up his bucket of water and walked quickly away.

Saul dismounted and yelled to Garf, 'If he's comin' here he ain't arrived yet.' Then he walked into the trees rimming the Lucky Bronco works, pulling his horse after him.

Cash stood quietly behind an oak as Saul settled down in a spot only a few feet from him. He drew his revolver and whispered, 'No noise, Saul.'

Saul whirled, his face twisted in fear and surprise.

'Neat,' said Cash. 'If I come around here, I'm supposed to go up to Garf while you put a slug in me from the trees.'

Saul turned away from Cash, who took Saul's gun from its holster and put it in the thick grass at his feet.

'Wait,' Saul said in a trembling voice. 'Remember what you said? I been doin' a lot of puzzlin' about that.' His face was lined in thought, yet as boyish as Hank had seen it when Saul was talking about Duke's gunplay.

'Make it short.'

'Like you said last night, you put all that to me too quick. But you were right. This game's no good. If I had me my chance right now, I'd light out for Wyoming and a straight puncher's life as fast as these boots would carry me.'

Cash frowned. 'That's quite a change of heart. Those

108

slugs you threw my way didn't sound half as reformed.'

'You switched around, didn't you? If one man can do it, another can. Ain't that right? Give me my chance!'

Cash glanced toward the mine. The chuckhouse had become as still as the empty buildings nearer the shaft. Garf and his horse had disappeared.

'Where's Garf gone?'

'No special place. He was supposed to bait you out if you was around here, just like you thought. Then I was supposed to knock you over from the trees with my rifle.' Saul's voice caught and he was almost in tears. 'He was makin' me do it! Leave me go just this once and I'll never show face around here again!'

Cash frowned briefly at the man before him. 'Some people I know are giving me a chance to help myself. I won't do less for you.'

A wide grin crinkled Saul's face. 'That's damned white of you.'

'Walk your animal north through these woods. And keep going.'

Saul heaved himself up into the saddle. He hesitated and said, 'I'm carryin' only that six-shooter you took off me. Can I have it back?'

'Hand me your gun belt.' Cash flipped the cylinder out and removed the shells. He took Saul's cartridge belt. 'Here. Take your gun. You can buy shells along the way. Good luck.'

Saul stuck the empty revolver in his belt and moved north through the trees at a slow walk. Soon he was out of sight.

Cash turned back to the mine. Garf was still not visible, hidden from view by the buildings around the shaft. Cash walked out of the trees and began to cross the open ground between the trees and the mine. He walked quietly, un-hurriedly, alert for any sign of Garf. He heard a horse snorting beyond the building nearest him and knew Garf was there.

From far off to his side there was the sudden, staccato thump of hoofs galloping over hard dirt. Saul's horse burst into the clearing at a dead run. He was riding with one foot in the stirrup, a hand gripping the saddlehorn, his body lowered and protected by the horse from Cash's line of fire. He bellowed, 'Garf! He's there behind the shack!'

Cash sprinted toward the wooden building as Saul disappeared on the far side of the chuckhouse. At the frame shack Cash waited, guns drawn, for Garf to show around one of the corners of the structure. He could hear Saul's horse stop on the far side. Saul said, 'Give me some shells!' Then there were low, excited whispers, and finally silence.

Cash edged around the building. From the corner he could see the two horses a few feet away, reins dropped to the ground. Saul and Garf had already disappeared.

The mine shaft several yards beyond the horses was littered with tools the miners had dropped to go to their noon meal. Rigged up over the large hole in the ground that was the shaft, was a long, thick wooden windlass with a heavy rope wrapped in tight coils around it. The lift. Cash could see no indication of the killers' hiding place. He stepped out into the open and walked slowly toward the shaft. His eyes and ears ached with the strain of trying to see and hear everything.

A dozen feet from the shaft he sensed a movement behind him and dodged, whirling around. A rifle cracked and the bullet whispered by his ear. He saw the glint of a barrel at the roof of the building he'd just circled and snapped a shot toward it. Then he turned and dived for an earth breastwork near the edge of the shaft as a second slug clanged through a shovel by his feet.

Crouched behind the four-foot earth wall, he turned back to the building. He had a glimpse of Garf's face over the roof as the gunman fired again, kicking up dirt in the top of Cash's natural barricade.

A shot from Cash's Colt splintered the wood where Garf's face had been a split second before.

Kneeling behind the wall of earth, Cash searched with narrowed eyes for Saul. Garf seemed to be alone on the roof of the building. Almost too late he understood the meaning of the whispers he'd heard. He twisted his head swiftly to see the tip of a revolver protruding up over the edge of the shaft behind him. His left arm squeezed up against the short dirt wall, he flipped an uncomfortable left-hand shot at the

110

barrel and it was jerked quickly back.

Saul's voice came up over the edge of the shaft to him. 'Too bad you saw me make my play. But never mind. I can stay standin' here on this platform all day waitin' for you to get careless. By God, we got you dead to rights. You come over toward me and Garf'll pick you off from that rooftop he's nestin' on. You turn to see what he's doin' and sooner or later I'll get you in the back.'

Cash inched out from the safety of the embankment toward the shaft. At the second step Garf sent a bullet whining near his head.

'See what I mean?' Saul chuckled, guessing what had happened.

Cash saw a long-handled ax lying a few feet away from him. He crept along the wall to where the bank tapered off and reached out gingerly for the handle. Garf didn't see what he was doing until the ax began moving as Cash hauled it in. A bullet from Garf's rifle slammed against the ax head, nearly ripping the tool from Cash's hand, then screamed angrily away into space.

Cash backed up to where he was nearest the windlass stretching over the shaft. He shifted the ax until it was in the best position. He swung his gun up to the edge of the embankment and sent two shots into the roof near Garf, who promptly ducked for cover. Then Cash grabbed the ax, leaped a short distance from cover and brought the sharp edge of the blade whistling down into the coils of the rope nearest him. He was back in the protection of the dirt wall before Garf peeked over the roof's edge again.

Saul said quickly, 'God damn! Whatcha – '

The rope on the windlass made a soft, popping sound and stretched, letting the platform down a sudden, bumping inch. Saul's two hands appeared above the edge of the large hole, one still gripping the revolver. The rope sputtered ominously and an instant later began whirling madly around the windlass. Saul's hand dropped the gun and he clung for a slipping moment to the dirt edge as the platform beneath him went rumbling swiftly down into the hole. Then his hands slipped away and he fell too, screaming in terror as he plunged far down into the deep pit. It seemed to Cash that Saul's high scream would never end. There

111

was a distant crash as the platform hit the bottom, and an instant later the screaming stopped.

Garf yelled from the roof, 'Saul! What happened? Saul!' He shouted twice more in rising panic, then stood up on the roof and walked down its gradual slope, firing as he came. Cash ducked, then glanced over the embankment as Garf balanced himself at the edge of the building, rifle in one hand, to jump down to where the horses were. Cash's slug hit him as he was about to leap. He swayed a moment on the roof, then leaned out and went down. Garf thudded onto Saul's pony, his stomach slamming onto the saddle-horn and his weight nearly throwing the mare's front legs out from under her. She gathered herself and raced wildly away. Garf's body rode a dozen feet before it slid on over the far side, rolling crazily as it pitched to the dusty ground.

Cash stood up as the door to the chuckhouse opened and two miners ran toward him. They stopped fifty feet away and one of them called, 'Is it all over?'

'Far as you fellows are concerned.'

The miner turned and yelled, 'Okay, you can come out now, boys.'

The other miners came swarming around the shaft, peering into the black depths below. A few walked out to look wide-eyed at Garf.

'You'll have to get a new rope and fix the platform,' Cash said as he reloaded his guns. 'Round up that runaway mare. Send the two bodies and the horses into Yellowrock with the next outbound wagon.' He walked through the crowded men and to Gold in the woods. He took the same short cut back to Yellowrock.

On First Street of the ghostlike town, Ma Bracken tapped on her new glass window to attract his attention. He brought Gold to a stand near her restaurant door. Ma came out the doorway and said, 'That pretty Virginia Brendan wasn't at work down to Clymer's.'

'Yes?'

'Well, I just put two and two together, Sheriff. I know Hall's tryin' to get you. Anyway, Ben had a cup of coffee and some beans in here for lunch and then went down to the Alamo where Hall is with Duke. A couple of minutes later he come ridin' in a hurry by here and headed out toward Spangle Valley.'

Cash spun Gold in a standing turn. The buckskin was in full gallop at its second stride.

CHAPTER TEN

Gold seemed to sense the urgent tension in Cash. The big stallion hurtled along the trail so swiftly that his hoofs seemed only rarely to touch the ground below, and then angrily, as though the momentary contact with the earth were a barrier to actual flight. His mane whipped in the wind as his shoulders butted ahead in tireless rhythm. Cash watched the ridges and horizons before him, hoping for a glance of Ben, hoping the big man would be riding slowly. Just once, as Gold plunged into the stream cutting through the bottom of Spangle Valley, clattering over its rocky bottom and sending torrents of spray to each side, he saw a single dot of a rider topping a far hill.

If that rider were Ben he would make it to Virginia's only two or three minutes before Cash. But in those two or three minutes – The muscles in Cash's shoulders tightened as he remembered the solid ash spoke Ben had ripped from the wagon wheel, the Mexican whose back Ben had broken as a normal man might break kindling wood. He remembered what Clymer had said: *She's not scared of many things, but she's scared of him.*

Gold felt the unconscious addition of leg pressure from his master and stretched his nose a little farther out as he thundered up a gradual incline and literally flew across the narrow ridge before plummeting down the far side.

When the buckskin leaped to the top of the last sharp hill and lunged down the long slope toward the distant house, Cash saw Ben's horse standing, still nervous, before the hitching-rack. Ben had evidently just dismounted. Virginia raced from the doorway and Ben, following, caught her in a few giant steps. He shook her roughly, tearing her dress, and turned as the pounding hoofbeats came nearer. Seeing Cash, he pulled Virginia to him, his arm around her neck.

Cash hauled Gold to a stop thirty feet away. Colt in hand he said, 'Let go of her.'

Ben took his time about answering. 'I ain't figuring you'll do nothin' much.' His deep voice was mocking and sure.

114

'If I was to move quick, it'd bust her neck sure. She's got such a little neck.'

'About the only thing I didn't peg you as was a coward.'

'I ain't. And I ain't as dumb as you take me for, neither. Duke could kill you with a gun, but I can't. Me, I been wantin' to do it with my hands. You throw down your guns and get off that horse and I'll leave her go.'

'No!' Virginia cried.

Cash thumbed his Colts to safety and dropped them to the soft ground. He dismounted.

Ben showed his yellow teeth in an ugly grin. 'That's right. Now we'll see – '

Virginia bit Ben's arm and tried to draw away. He snarled in pain and slapped her from him. Under the impact of his great hand, she fell and lay still. Cash saw Hank appear from the woods, running at top speed straight toward Ben.

'Keep away from him!' Cash ordered sharply.

Hank stopped, his eyes blazing.

'Look to your mother,' Cash said.

Ben pulled his revolver and waved it toward the house. 'Step away from where your guns lay. Git over there.'

Cash backed toward the porch and Ben followed, slowly replacing his gun. 'Now I'm gonna break your back. Then I'll pull your ears off.'

The big man crouched and moved in on Cash, his arms outstretched. Cash backed two steps as the arms came closer, then stepped quickly in and lashed out with all his strength at Ben's face. He felt the skin of his knuckles break, felt the bones in his fingers and clear up to his elbow almost give beneath the jarring force of the blow. Ben's head jerked back and he staggered slightly. Then he caught himself and grinned. 'Figure that's about as hard as you can hit. And it don't bother me none at all. You're done.'

Cash retreated as the giant moved toward him once again. Then his back came up against the corner of the house. Ben lunged at him. Cash grabbed the big man's hair, tearing the huge head up at an angle as Ben came in to catch him. Then he drove his knee high and hard into Ben's exposed throat. Ben gurgled in agony, but his

115

momentum drove Cash into the frame wall behind him with the force of a horse's whirling hindquarters. The wind knocked out of him, Cash fought for breath as Ben crashed on by him, losing his gun from its holster. Ben rolled on the ground, then raised himself on one knee, glaring at Cash and rubbing his throat.

Cash edged toward his guns. Seeing this, Ben jumped to cut him off, his hand instinctively groping for his own revolver.

'You haven't got one, either,' Cash whispered.

'Won't need it.' Ben shifted to work Cash back toward the house and the barn beyond it. Cash backed around the corner of the house toward the barn. Ben suddenly rushed him again and Cash ducked to one side. Instead of trying to wrap his arms around him, Ben struck out with his huge fist. The powerful blow caught Cash's left shoulder, spinning him around and throwing him to the ground. The wound in his arm was torn open again and he could feel blood soaking through the bandage. Cash saw Ben leaping at him and rolled as a huge boot crunched viciously into the dirt where his head had been. Then Cash was on his feet, running toward the barn. Ben lumbered after him.

In the barn Cash stooped quickly and reached down with his good right hand to tear the spur from his boot. As Ben rounded the corner of the barn and rushed in the door, Cash struck out with his fist doubled over one shank of the spur. The sharp rowels slashed across Ben's forehead, opening deep gouges in the skin as the giant ducked. Cash backed again, the spur still clutched in his hand.

Ben hesitated and blinked the welling blood away from his eyes. A short chain was hanging near him. He reached out and snatched it from its peg. Slowly and methodically he twisted the chain around his hand. When he had finished, his clenched fist looked like a small keg wrapped until it was hidden with heavy links of steel. 'I'll cut you up before I kill you,' he muttered. 'I owe it to you now.'

Cash leaped in again and swung up at the narrowed eyes. The spur connected with Ben's head and grated against bone as it plowed across his forehead. Ben answered the blow with a short, chopping punch with the chained fist that slammed against Cash's head and sent him sprawling onto the barn floor.

116

Cash twisted back onto his feet instantly, but before he could get away Ben grabbed his shoulder and spun him into the grip of those mighty arms. Cash gasped as the power in Ben surged up through the great shoulders and arms and began to crush the life from him. His own arms were caught between him and Ben. With all his strength he pushed his right arm up. As the blackness was coming he saw that his spur rowel was on a level with Ben's nearly closed eyes. Using all the power he could gather, he twisted his wrist sharply, plunging the rowel into Ben's right eye. Ben screamed and released his grip slightly. Cash brought his knee up into the big man's groin. There was a second cry of agony and the tremendous arms were released altogether. Cash stumbled away as Ben slumped to his knees and grasped at his blinded eye.

The strong man knelt there only a few seconds. Then he was up again, wiping the blood from his good eye, searching for Cash. Cut off from the door, Cash slowly backed away. His shoulder touched a beam and he moved aside. In the shadows of the barn, his eyesight betraying him, Ben mistook the beam for Cash and struck out with his chained fist. The beam shook under the crunching thud and marks of the chain's links showed in the wood. Ben grunted in pain and drew back his hand, still moving forward. He struck again as Cash dodged and the mighty fist snapped a smaller log bracing the beam.

Cash drove his own fist swiftly into Ben's throat, the bloodied spur tearing deeply into the flesh, and it was then that the giant went mad. He roared with insane fury and began to lash out blindly with wild, shattering blows. His naked fist shot out almost invisibly and crashed into Cash's chest, knocking him down. The great fist with the chain followed in a wide arc that slashed through the air where Cash had been and crashed on into the wall of the barn like a battering ram, smashing a hole through it.

Cash dropped the spur as Ben, screaming and cursing incoherently, staggered toward where he had fallen. Rolling to his feet, Cash ducked away. He was now in the corner near the stalls where the fencing equipment was stored. On a shelf to his right were the piled bales of barbed wire. Cash kicked a support out from under the shelf and the heavy wire slithered to the barn floor, several loops springing open as it rolled and fell.

Ben charged straight into the wicked barrier and fell headlong as his foot tripped on the first roll of needle-sharp points. His clothes and flesh ripped and torn by the barbs, he struggled to free himself from the tangled mass of fencing. Pain meant nothing to him any longer. As Cash retreated, trying to save some of his fading strength, Ben seemed suddenly to have reached his greatest power.

He picked up a great ball of wire in his left hand and threw it from him, leaving his hand invisible behind the blood that gushed out of a hundred gashes. He kicked and screamed and fought his way through the maze of wire toward Cash. He decided to get rid of the chain on his right hand and began unwinding it. It twisted and stuck at one point and he shrieked with rage and hunched his shoulders to snap the balky chain in two. Then he was through the wire. He wiped his hand over his good eye and dimly saw Cash trapped, backing up toward the end of a stall. He charged at him.

Cash picked up a sharpened iron stake from the stack of them leaning against the barn wall as he retreated into the stall. His back was almost to the wall when Ben came at him. His left arm and hand were useless and his right hand was numb. He could hardly lift the stake. As Ben raged into the stall, Cash eased back against the wall. With what little strength he had, he swung the stake up with his right hand so that its end was braced against the wall and under his armpit. The sharpened point facing Ben wavered uncertainly as he tried to hold it steady. The stake was starting to slip from his fingers when Ben ran, chest on, against its point. As the giant impaled himself, one of his huge hands crashed into Cash's head and knocked him down once more.

Cash opened his eyes to find Ben lying near him.

Although he'd died almost instantly, Ben's great hands had knotted themselves about the stake in an effort to pull it from his chest.

Cash struggled to his feet. At the door to the barn he leaned his right hand on the frame and took several deep gulps of air. Then, his left hand hanging limply at his side, he walked slowly toward the house.

Hank sat on the ground with his mother's head cradled in his lap. 'She won't open her eyes or say nothin' at all,' he said softly. 'And I thought you were gonna be killed. And I didn't care if that big man came back and got me, too.'

Cash put his hand on Virginia's chest and could feel a light but regular heartbeat. She was breathing faintly. 'I think she'll be all right, Hank. If we hitch up the buckboard do you think you could go into town and get Joe Gaines?'

'Sure.'

'First, help me get her inside.' Cash got his right arm under Virginia and lifted her against his chest, using strength he didn't know he had.

When she was put comfortably on the bunk inside, Hank helped Cash hitch Lightning to the buckboard and the boy drove at a fast, confident clip away from the house. Cash went back in and sat beside Virginia. In time she began to breathe more deeply and with firm regularity. Cash got up and went outside for his guns. He snapped the cylinders out with his one good hand and examined the barrels. They were clean. He flipped the cylinders back in and holstered the guns. . . .

It was nearly dusk when the familiar whirring of the wheels on the light rig came again to Cash's ears. Through the window he could see Hank pull up in the front yard while Joe Gaines jumped down and hurried to the front door. He came in and said, 'How is she?'

'Breathing's got a little better since the boy left.'

As Joe bent over Virginia he said, 'We come lickety-split up the road. That boy drives like a top whip on the Grand-ville Stage. We saw Whitey Hall and Duke takin' off at a calm pace through the hills toward here. They can't be more'n a mile or so distant right now.'

Cash went to the front of the house and said, 'You made good time.'

Hank came up to the porch. 'Is she doin' any better?'

'I think she'll be all right.'

'Did he tell you about them two we saw?'

'Yes.'

'They comin' for you?'

Cash nodded. 'Come on in and we'll see about your mother.'

Gaines got up as they entered. 'She'll be comin' around pretty quick. Minor concussion. What happened to Ben?'

'He's out in the barn.'

'Dead?'

'Yes.'

'You look pretty close to that yourself.' Gaines's eyes went from Cash's bruised face to his lifeless arm. 'Kid says he made you throw down your guns. How'd you come by one to finish him?'

'I didn't. He tripped over some barbed wire and fell on a fence stake.'

'Just like that?'

Cash looked down at Virginia. 'Take good care of her.' He walked to the door.

'You goin' out to meet them?' Gaines asked.

'That's right.'

'You can sit tight right here if you want. Coach came in from the mines this afternoon. Brought in Saul and Garf. Now that you got the ball rollin' and the odds cut down, the town's in an uproar. They're out to get Whitey for what he tried to do to Williams. And some old-timer in town says he knew Whitey Hall all along from back in Dodge City or someplace. Said Hall was thrown in jail by that sheriff named Sullivan – the same as got shot before you took office. And Hap Borland stepped up and said you and him knew Whitey was crooked, too. Said you just took the job to get a line on Hall and his men.'

'Hap Borland said that?'

'Yep. Said to be sure to tell you if I saw you. And, to get to the point, a whole bunch of men were saddlin' up to take out after Whitey and Duke when me and Hank left.'

'That's fine. But I'll finish my own fight.'

'You need some help,' Hank insisted.

Cash went out the door.

He caught Gold and swung into saddle. The sun was out of sight when he started up the valley slope. He had a fleeting glimpse of the rim of the great, warm ball from the top of the ridge before it disappeared. In the gathering purple shadows a few minutes later he saw two riders coming over a distant bluff.

He let Gold pick his way down the slope at a walk. When

120

he hit level ground the two riders coming toward him were almost into a large cove of trees. Moments later they emerged on the near side and Cash could see that it was Whitey and Duke. Whitey pulled his mount to a halt and Duke rode on alone, slowly.

Duke was sitting straight in the saddle, his wiry shoulders squared against the shifting muscles of his horses's back. He looked strong and confident and his hand was not yet near his gun. Cash felt suddenly weak and hopeless as he recalled the blurring speed of Duke's gunplay. The weight of his hanging left arm dragged down on his left shoulder and the wound burned now as though a branding iron had just been removed from it. Along with Duke's gunplay, though, he remembered Duke's words – words that had pricked the emotional armour of a professional fighter and had made him nervous for one crucial second.

Cash waited until Duke was in shouting distance. Then he called, 'Duke.'

Duke's eyes didn't leave him. He let his horse move on at the same, unhurried pace. 'Yeah?'

'You must be feeling bad. No audience.'

'I feel okay.'

'That's the way Ben felt.'

Duke's left hand was holding the reins. The hand lifted slightly. That was the only change. 'You kill Ben?'

'Sure. And Saul. And Garf. And Lewt. And now it's your turn, Duke. It's getting to be downright monotonous.' Cash could see that Duke was not affected by that line of talk. He made a wild guess. 'You'll be a dead cinch on a horse.'

Duke's hand tightened on the reins and his animal stopped three hundred feet from where Cash sat Gold. 'What are you talkin' about?'

'You never fought from horseback. There's a trick to it. It's an old Comanche trick you pick up poppin' brush in the wild horse country. I'd tell you about it, except that pretty soon you won't be around any more to use it.'

Duke hesitated. 'You picked up the idea of throwin' a scare into the other man from watchin' me fight Griggs. You're bluffin'.'

'I'm glad you think so, Duke. But the truth is, sitting right there where you are, you're a dead man. You try to

121

swing down and I'll kill you before yourt foot touches ground. You keep coming and I'll show you how the trick works.'

Cash could see Duke was no longer so sure of himself. The faint smile the slender gunman had worn while facing Matt Griggs was gone. The light of pleasure was not in his eyes. Duke touched his mount's flanks and moved slowly forward again, his lips and jaw firmly set, his eyes narrowed and watching intently for anything that Cash might try.

'Trouble is, Duke,' Cash said, his voice carrying clearly through the still mountain dusk, 'you can't see a thing to give away this trick. That's why the Comanches liked it.'

Duke was a hundred feet away, moving steadily forward.

'A little farther, Duke.' Cash's voice was now low and soothing. His legs tightened imperceptibly on Gold.

Gold put back an inquiring ear as the pressure increased, then pointed both ears back at the approaching rider and horse. Duke missed that single movement, which might have signalled the danger to him.

Cash's voice was almost crooning now. 'What do you think it can be, Duke? Enough to make a man nervous, isn't it? What will it be like to die?'

The gentle voice had dropped to little more than an audible whisper. Duke's hand had moved close to his gun, but in the fading light Cash could no longer read the message in Duke's eyes.

Sixty feet. Now Duke would be expecting to get in to closer fighting quarters. Now was the time. 'Poor Duke,' Cash added in a quiet, almost purring voice.

Then, from high in his throat, Cash screamed a piercing, high-pitched shriek that cut through the air like a thrown knife. Following so suddenly and viciously on top of the soft voice, it made Duke's horse throw its head and neck back in a startled, frightened, half-rear. Duke instinctively jerked hard on the reins, sending the spooked horse into a plunging buck as it tried to get hold of the cutting bit.

Gold's muscles tensed as the cry filled his ears, but the controlling pressure was already there and the buckskin stood still, his flesh trembling slightly.

Cash went for his gun at the moment the war whoop started. The Colt jumped swiftly into his hand. Duke was having trouble, but his right hand acted like a separate part of him. His Smith & Wesson appeared over the pommel of his saddle with the speed of a striking rattler.

The two forty-fives roared almost together and their double echoes rolled across the valley and into the hills. Cash felt as if a great fist had slammed into his shoulder and sent him spinning backwards. The whole world went into a short, violent arc and he found himself stretched out in the dirt, staring up at Gold and the darkening sky beyond the horse's body.

Duke sat his now quieted horse and gazed in the direction of the figure on the ground. Slowly he returned his gun to its holster.

'Duke!' Now that the shooting was over, Whitey spurred his horse toward the scene of the gun duel. He came abreast of Duke and pulled his mount up. 'That damned yell made my own mare act up clear back there. He nearly had you on that.'

'Yeah,' Duke whispered. 'Nearly.'

Duke sighed deep in his stomach and the end of the sigh turned into a grating noise that was almost like humourless laughter. He leaned toward Hall and put out a hand as though he wanted something to hold on to. He didn't stop leaning. His body arched out of the saddle and he fell on the side of his face, his left foot caught in the stirrup.

Hall jumped down from his mare and hurried toward the fallen man. Duke's horse, still flighty, sidestepped two paces, dragging Duke with him. Then Hall caught the stirrup and snatched away the boot caught in it.

'Duke?' Hall bent down. 'Duke. You get hit?' He was silent for a minute. Then he called loudly, as though commanding an answer, 'Duke! Duke!'

Finally he stood up and went to his mare. Gathering the reins in his hand he led her toward where Cash lay. Cash could see him coming, could see him take out his gun as he approached. Cash had just enough strength to close the fingers of his right hand.

But the hand was empty. He had dropped the gun in falling.

Hall stood over him and peered down in the dark shadows now covering the ground. 'You're still alive.'

Cash's throat and tongue were dry. He tried to speak but could not.

'I always planned that either Duke or Ben would have the pleasure of killing you,' Hall continued. 'But things change. Now I get to do it.'

The moon moved over a faraway peak, casting a silver blanket of cold light. Cash could see Hall raising his revolver. He managed to say, 'Go ahead. I've already done more – more than I thought I could do.'

'Done what?' Hall demanded, his voice shaking with fury. 'You've ruined me and got yourself killed! That's what you've done. What for? For your conscience? For the people in Yellowrock? Are they here now that you need them? You're alone, and not one person will help you in return!' Whitey's hand trembled as he put away his gun. His voice was low, fierce with intensity. 'Shooting isn't enough. I prefer a blade for you.' He took a knife from its scabbard on his belt and leaned toward Cash.

A shot blasted the short silence and Whitey was rocked back on his heels, his arms flying up. Cash watched him as he struggled briefly for balance, then buckled and fell to one side.

He could hear light, running footsteps and then Hank was leaning down over his chest, the Spencer Cash had given him clutched tightly in one hand. The boy was weeping and near hysteria. 'I had to do it,' he cried. 'There was nothing else to do. I had to do it!'

Cash gritted his teeth with the effort and brought his arm up to hold the boy's shoulder as Hank sobbed on his chest. . . .

Later, Hank forced himself to be calm. He said, 'Are you hurt bad? Will you be okay?'

'Yes. I'll be fine. Give me a minute to breathe.'

Hank ran his fingers over Cash. 'You got it on that same shoulder again. Higher and deeper into the arm.'

'Come on. Let's see if we can get me up.' Cash turned onto his good shoulder and shifted unsteadily onto his feet, Hank helping him.

Hank walked into the dark and brought Gold back to where Cash was standing, getting the feel of his muscles. Cash hauled himself into the saddle and, his jaw tensed against the pain, pulled Hank up in front of him.

'I thought I never would catch up to you,' Hank said as

124

the buckskin started up toward the hill silhouetted dimly ahead. 'I started out wrong. Got clear across the river when I heard guns back this way. Runnin' back through the river I slipped and fell down. Kept my rifle up, all right, but I lost what I was holdin' in my other hand.'

'What was that?'

'Sullivan's badge. Your badge. The water took it and it's a hard current there. It's gone.' The boy leaned back against Cash, suddenly tired. 'It's gone.'

'It doesn't matter.'

'I guess you're right,' Hank agreed.

At the house Hank leaped to the ground. Joe Gaines came out as Cash let himself down. 'I never saw a man so beat up and still walkin'.'

Virginia opened her eyes while Gaines was boiling one pot of water to clean Cash's wounds, and another for coffee. She stretched out her hand to Cash and he took it and sat on the edge of the bunk.

'Is it all over?' she asked in a small voice.

Cash nodded.

'Couple of times there,' Gaines said from the stove, 'I thought we'd be needin' a new sheriff.'

'You would have, save for this boy,' Cash said.

Two horses could be heard trotting up outside, and Gaines went out to meet the riders. He returned and said, 'They was part of the main bunch out lookin' for Duke and Whitey. I told them it was all over but the cleanin' up, and they're gonna get to that directly.'

'They have any late word on Williams?' Cash asked.

Joe seemed to be embarrassed. He turned to where Cash was sitting beside Virginia. 'From the way they said it, I don't know if he was out of his head or not. Anyway's, they said he woke up and said he was gonna get up and around in time to marry you two. He must have been talkin' wild, to tell a thing like that around that way so's the whole town would be in on it.'

Virginia smiled. 'I'm glad we're in on it too.'

Hank said, 'I already told Ma, Cash, that we ought to build an extra room and have you stay with us.'

'Would it be all right,' Virginia asked, 'if we made that extra room for you, Hank, instead of for Cash?'

'Well,' Hank said, 'I guess so. Sure. Any way you want to fix it will be okay with me.'

THE END

TERRY HARKNETT
CROWN
The Sweet & Sour Kill

Hong Kong: Where East meets West in a boom city of skyscrapers and shanty towns, of luxury hotels and sleazy waterfront bars. Where anything can be had for a price, from a pretty girl to a shipment of raw heroin.

When an American mob, backed with Mafia money, muscle in on the colony's lucrative rackets, offering their special brand of 'protection', they were trespassing on Crown's patch.

Chief Superintendent John Crown wasn't an orthodox policeman. Tough, bitter and ruthless, he believed that bullets spoke louder than words, and some of his methods weren't listed in any police manual.

And he had a special dislike for trespassers.

ESCAPE FROM THE RISING SUN
IAN SKIDMORE

'The oily dust fell everywhere, on hungry
stragglers searching for their units, on armed
deserters who roamed the streets searching for
loot, on . . . fear-crazed men fighting their way
at the point of a gun or bayonet, pushing women
and children aside . . . The dead lay in the
streets . . . but no one collected the corpses now'

Singapore had fallen. The British Army, retreating
in disorder before the onslaught of the Japanese
shock-troops, had been told to surrender. One
man was convinced he could escape.

Geoffrey Rowley-Conwy seized a junk and sailed
for Padang. There he joined a group of fellow
officers for a desperate escape-bid in a dilapidated
sailing boat across the Indian Ocean to Ceylon.
1,500 miles of open sea swept by the fury of the
monsoon and patrolled by Japanese fighter planes
on the lookout for British survivors.

'One of the best and liveliest escape stories of
the Second World War . . . enthralling.'
Times Literary Supplement